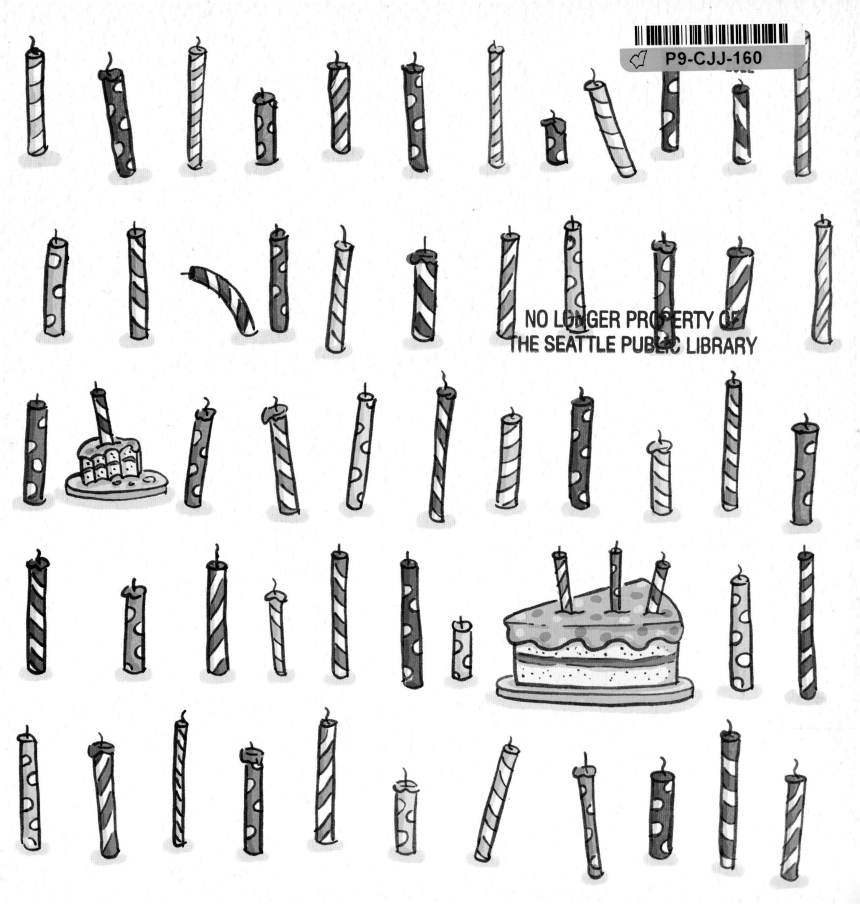

P9-CJJ-160

NO LONGER PROPERTY OF
THE SEATTLE PUBLIC LIBRARY

For my extraordinary agent, Jen, who is proof that making a wish when you blow out your birthday candles totally works —D.P.

To DT, TH, BF & PB for always eating cake with me —R.C.

The art in this book was created with India ink and digital color.

Library of Congress Control Number 2021937062

ISBN 978-1-4197-4670-3

Text © 2022 Dev Petty
Illustrations © 2022 Ruth Chan
Book design by Brenda E. Angelilli and Pamela Notarantonio

Published in 2022 by Abrams Books for Young Readers, an imprint of ABRAMS. All rights reserved. No portion of this book may be reproduced, stored in a retrieval system, or transmitted in any form or by any means, mechanical, electronic, photocopying, recording, or otherwise, without written permission from the publisher.

Printed and bound in China
10 9 8 7 6 5 4 3 2 1

Abrams Books for Young Readers are available at special discounts when purchased in quantity for premiums and promotions as well as fundraising or educational use. Special editions can also be created to specification. For details, contact specialsales@abramsbooks.com or the address below.

Abrams® is a registered trademark of Harry N. Abrams, Inc.

ABRAMS The Art of Books
195 Broadway, New York, NY 10007
abramsbooks.com

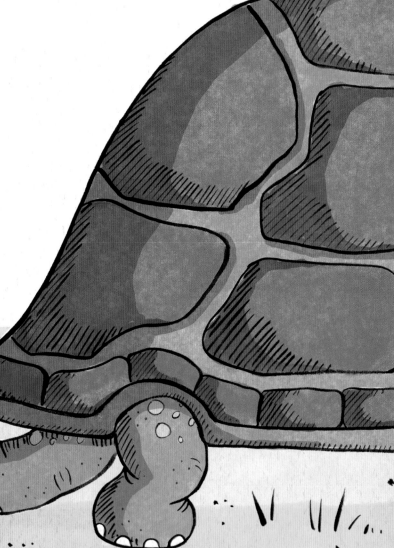

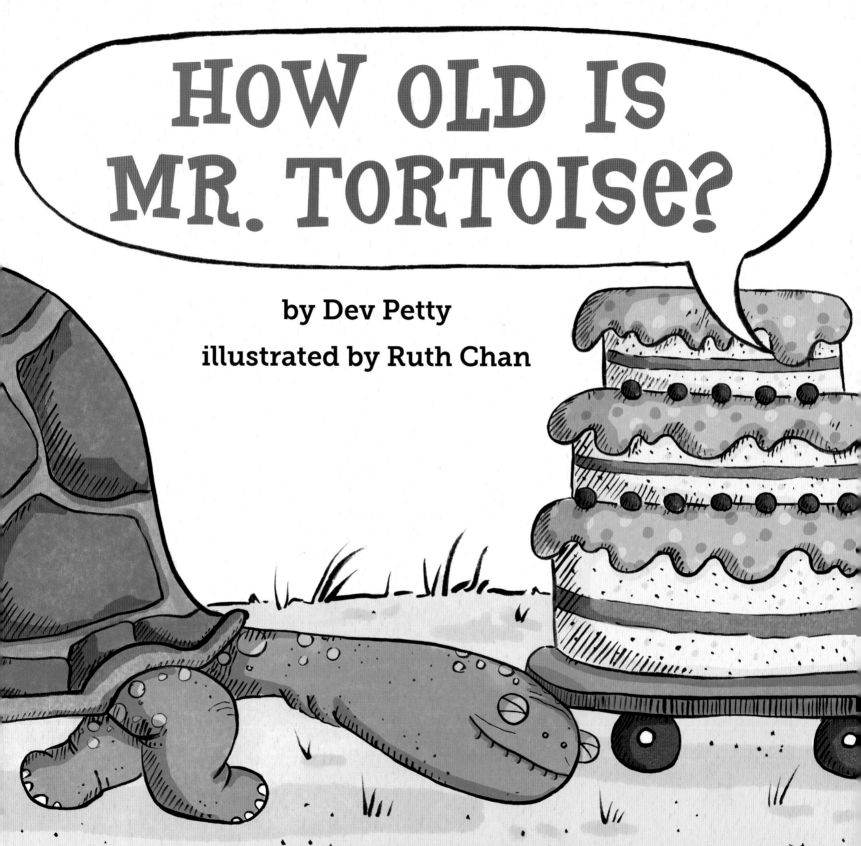

HOW OLD IS MR. TORTOISE?

by Dev Petty

illustrated by Ruth Chan

Abrams Books for Young Readers • New York

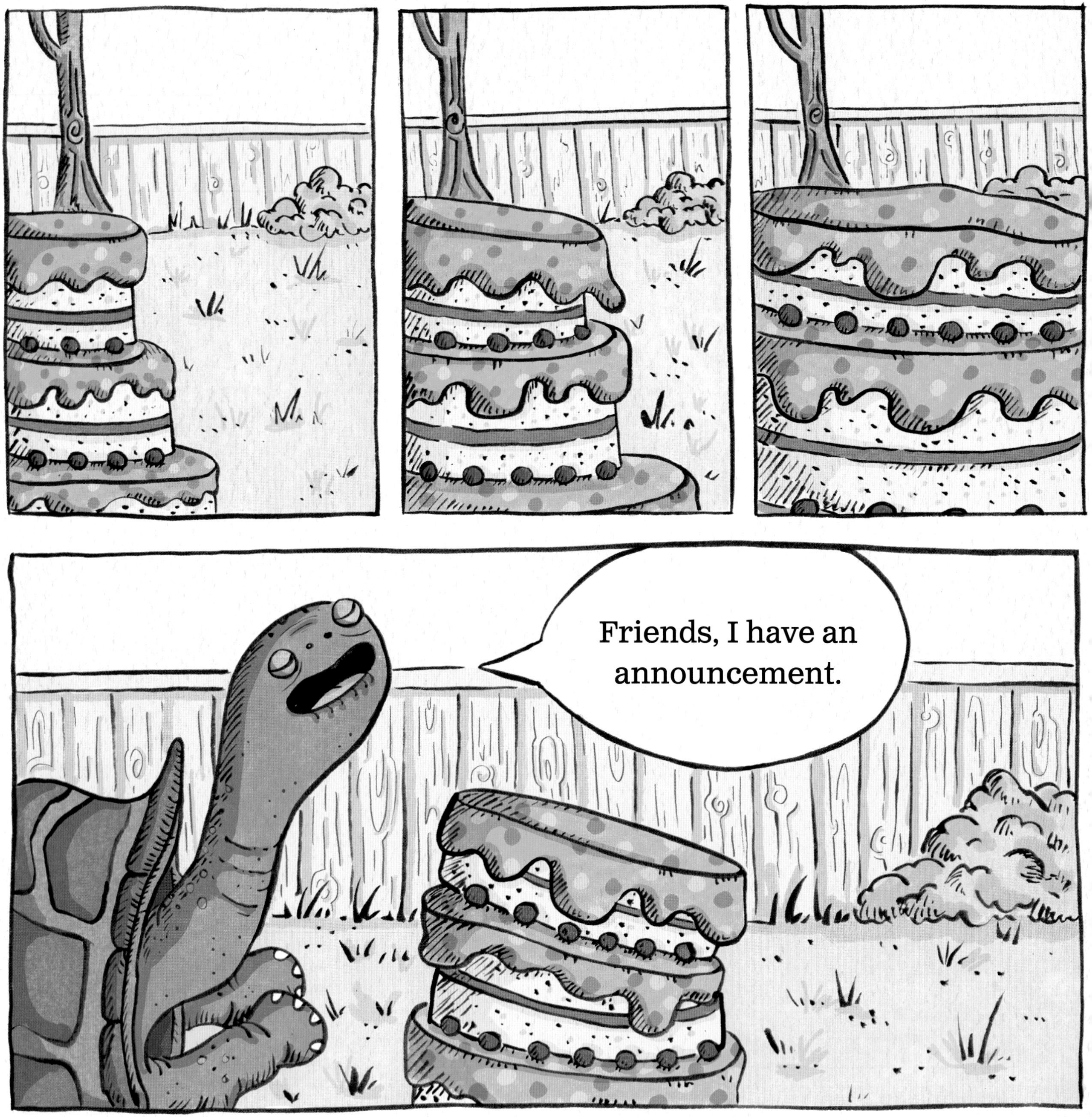
Friends, I have an announcement.

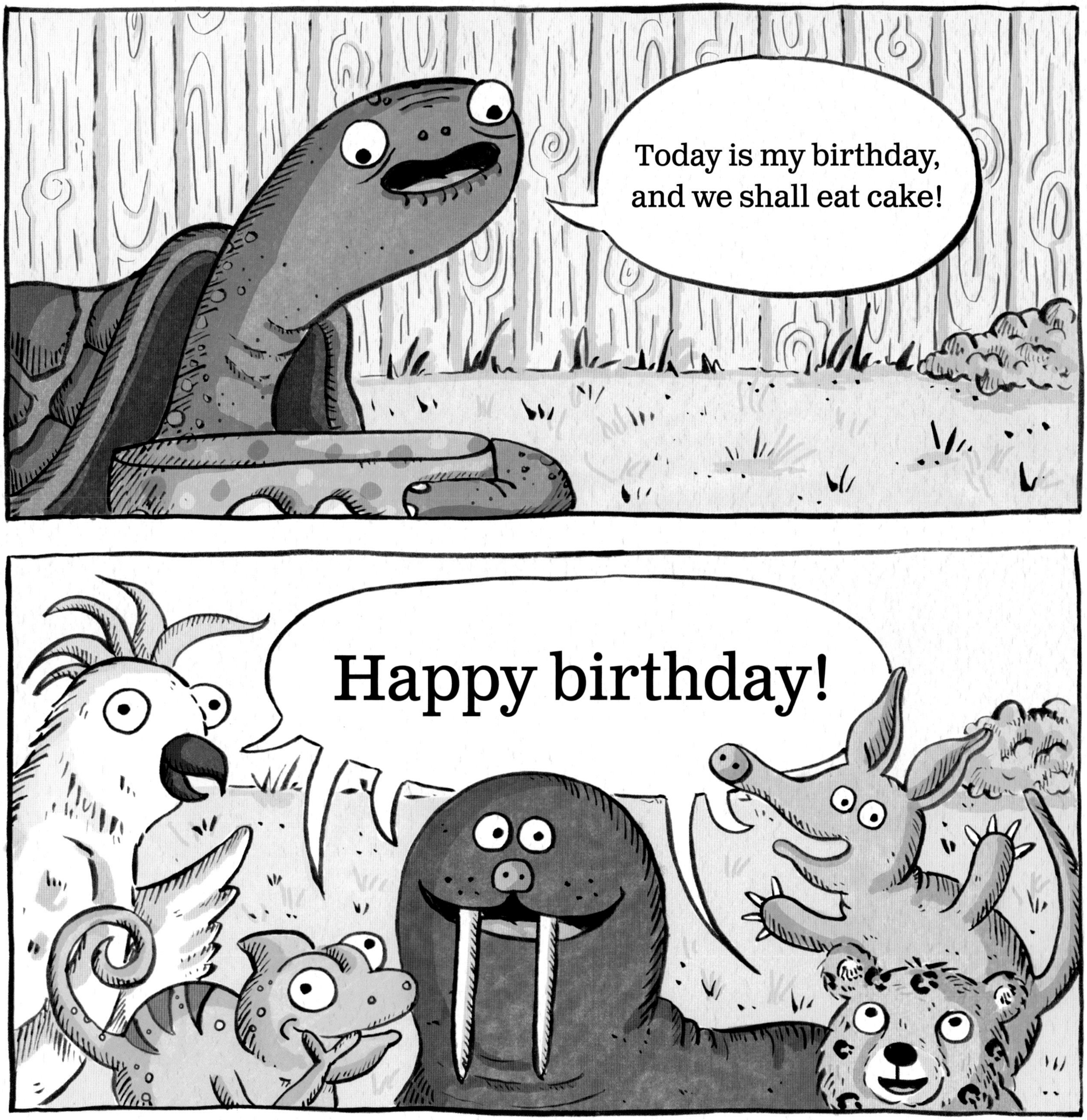
Today is my birthday, and we shall eat cake!
Happy birthday!

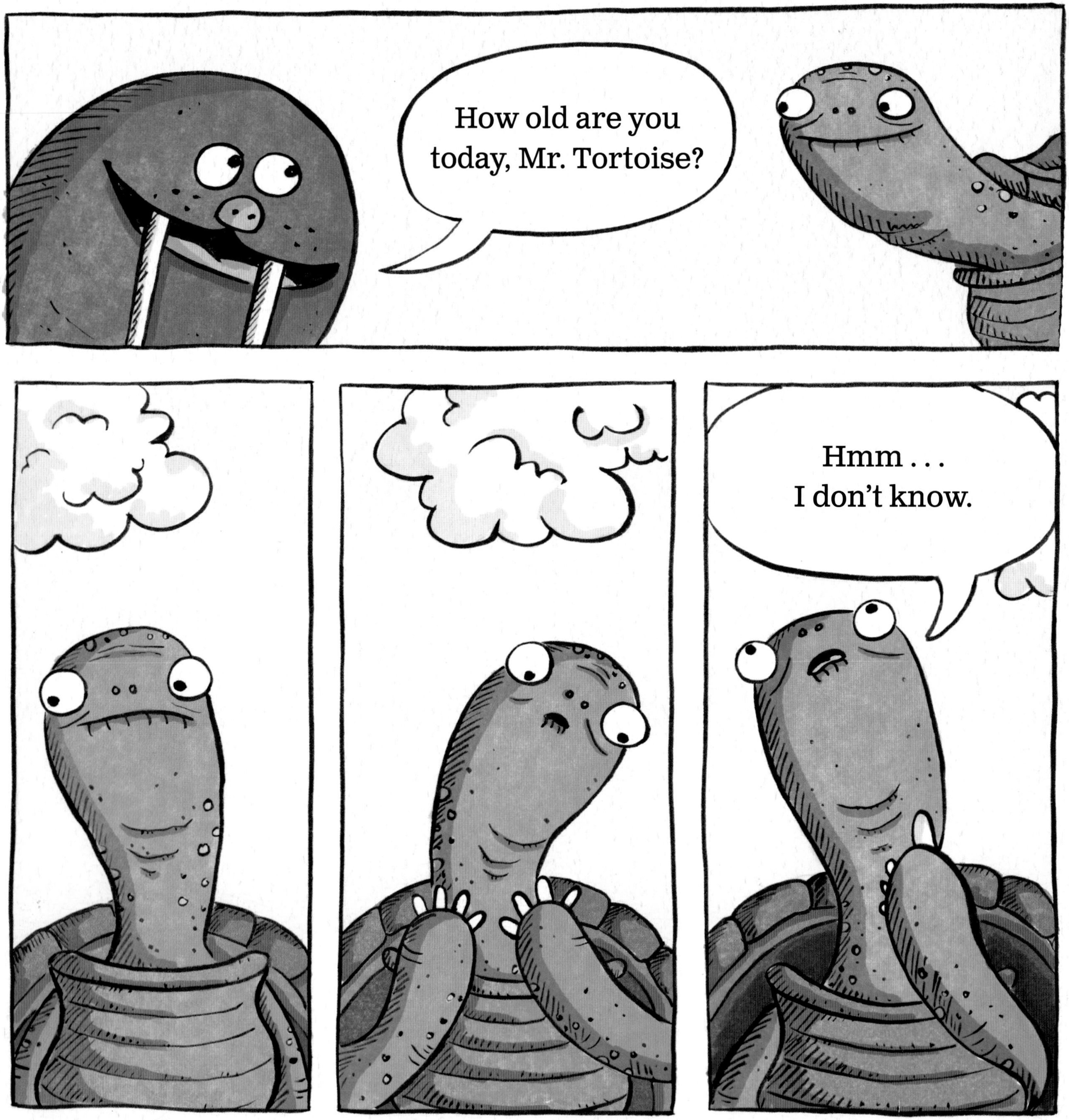
How old are you today, Mr. Tortoise?
Hmm . . . I don’t know.

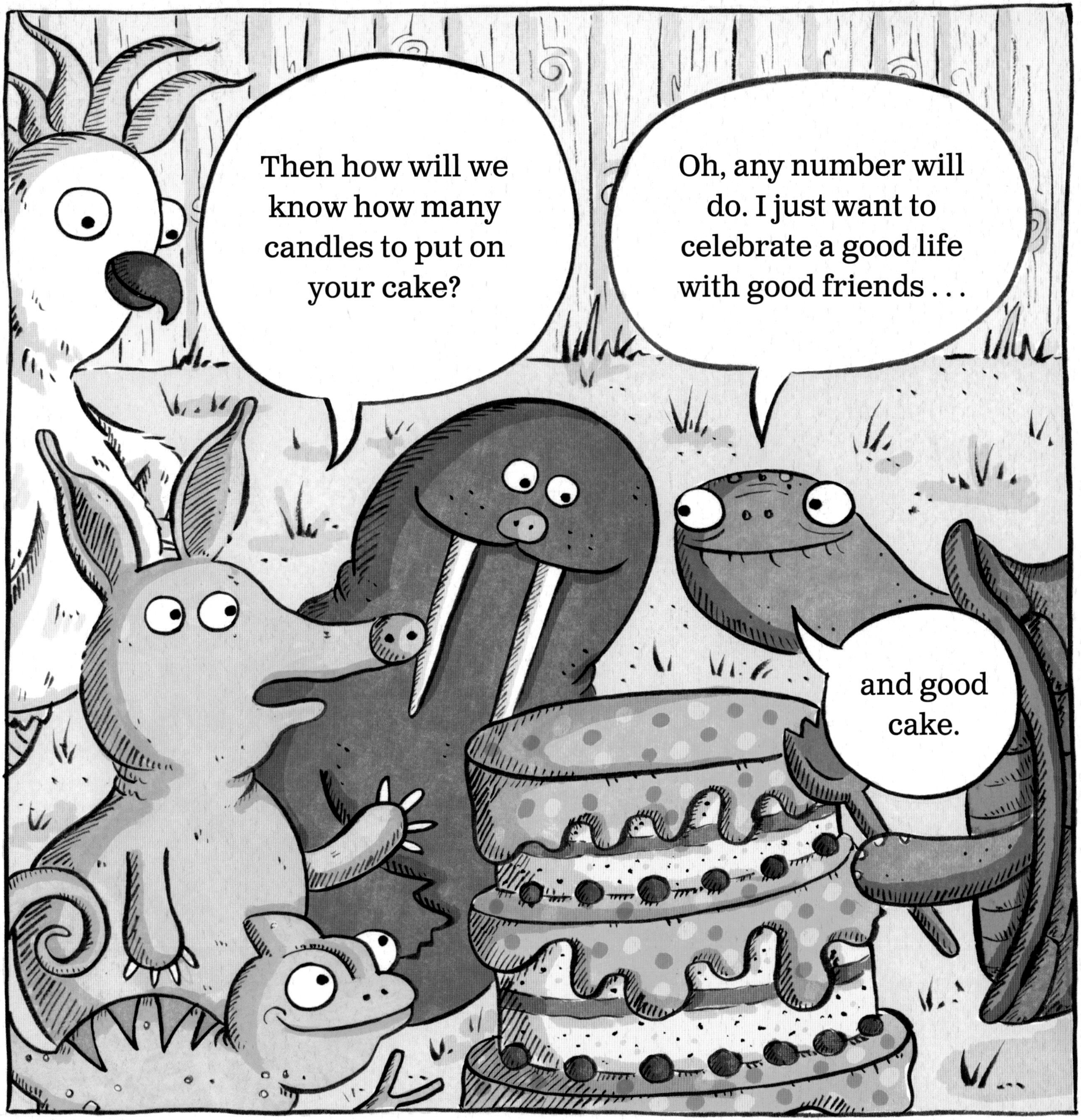
Then how will we know how many candles to put on your cake?
Oh, any number will do. I just want to celebrate a good life with good friends . . .
and good cake.

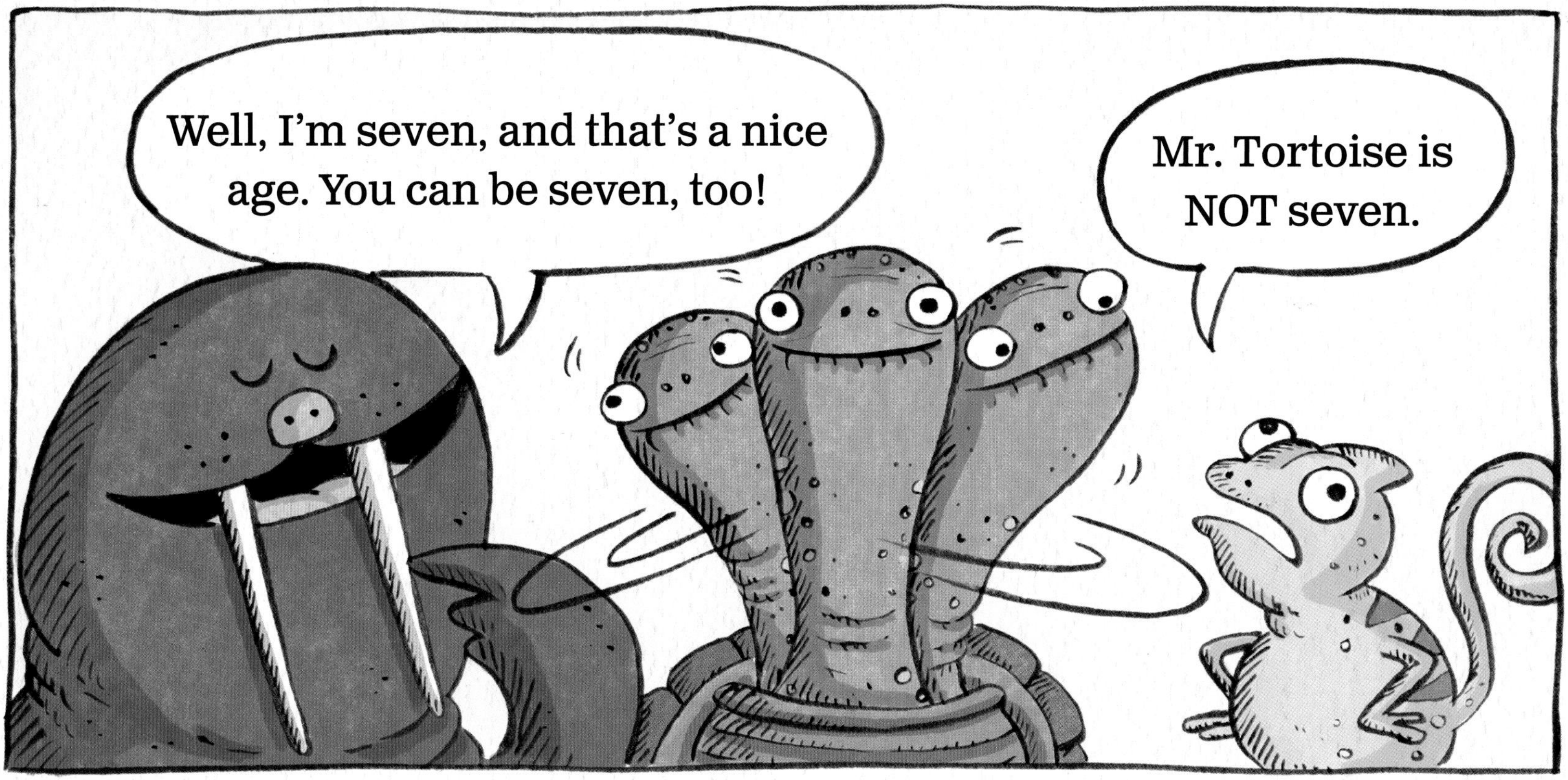
Well, I'm seven, and that's a nice age. You can be seven, too!
Mr. Tortoise is NOT seven.

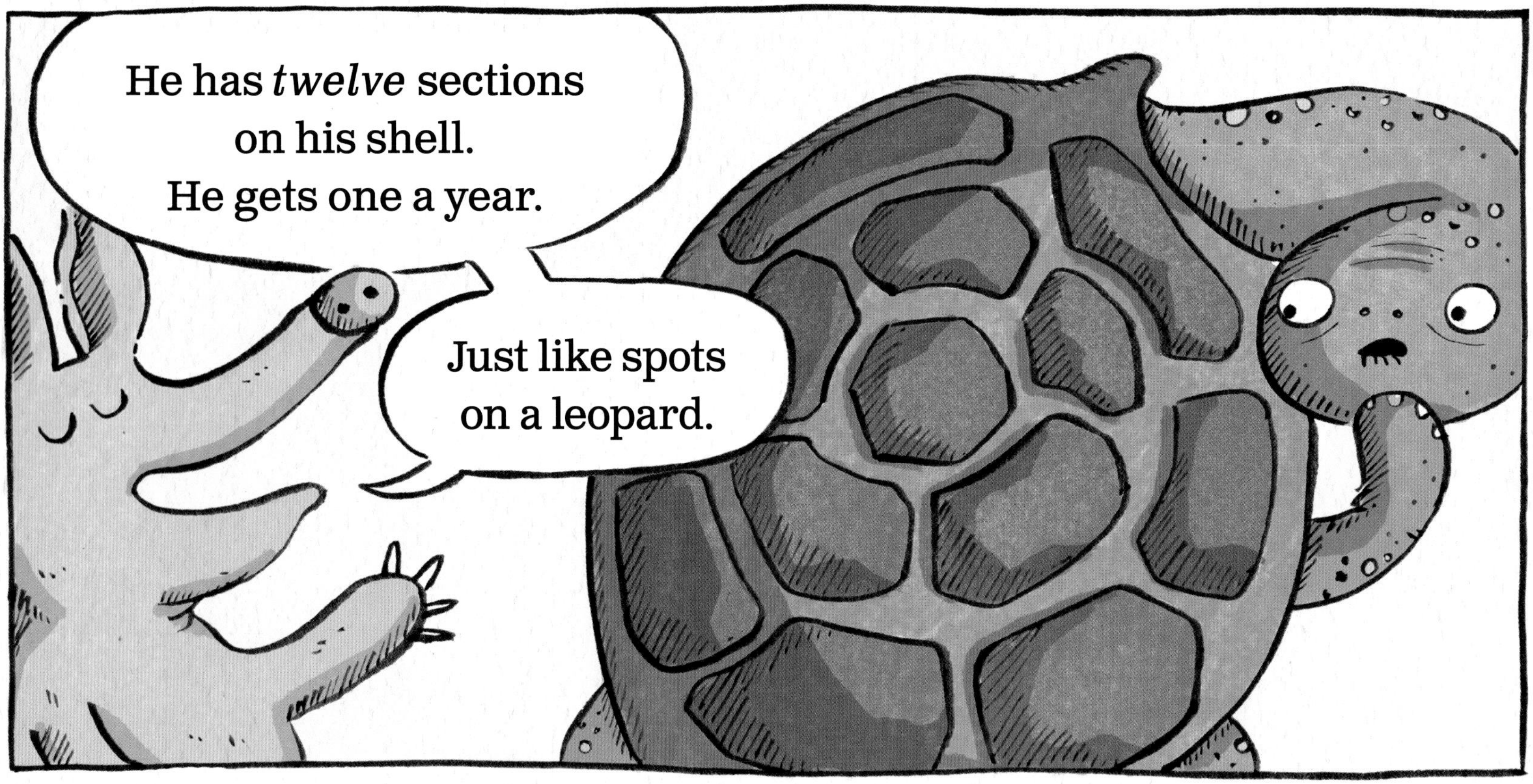
He has *twelve* sections on his shell. He gets one a year.
Just like spots on a leopard.

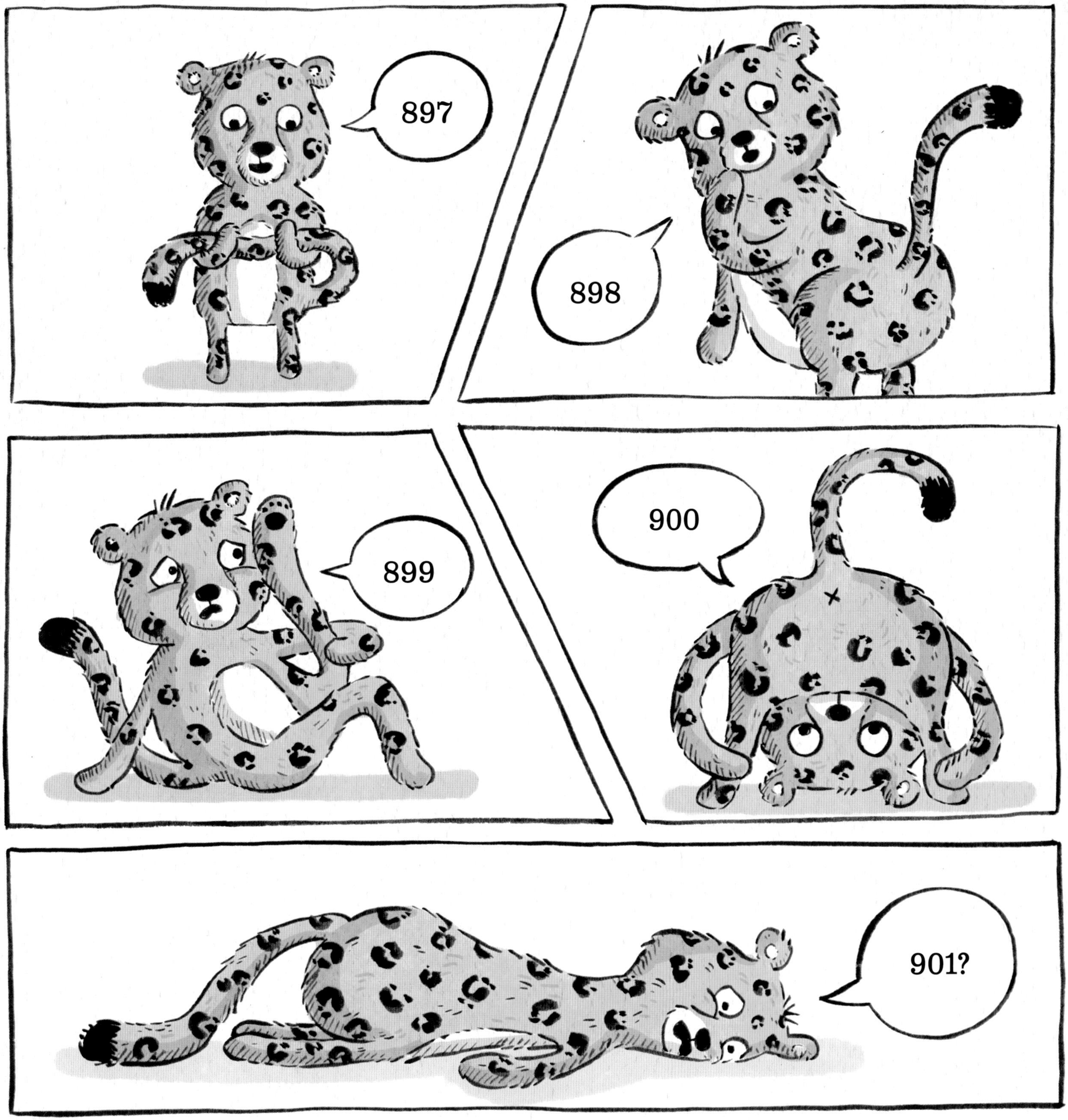
897
898
899
900
901?

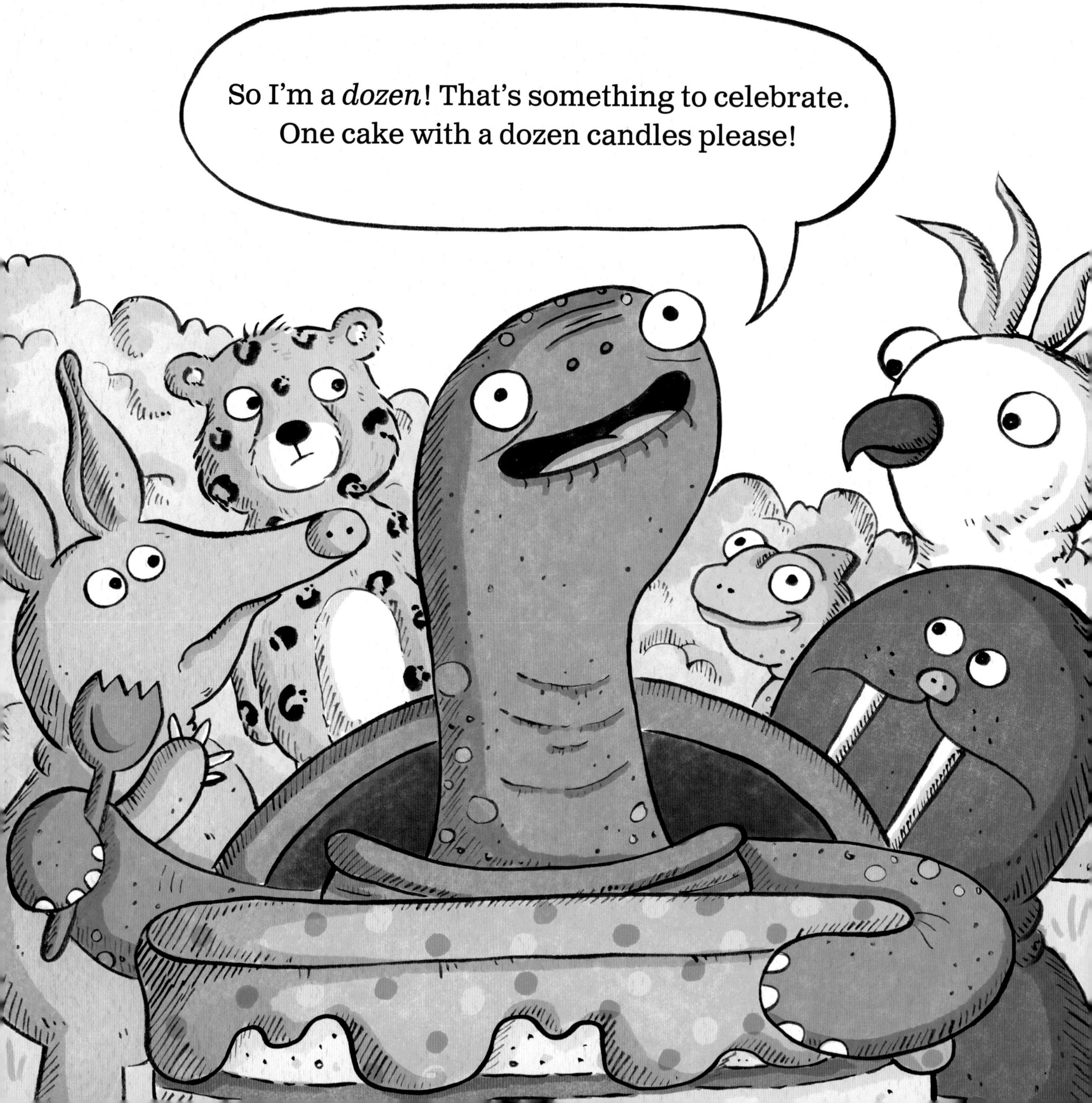
So I'm a *dozen*! That's something to celebrate. One cake with a dozen candles please!

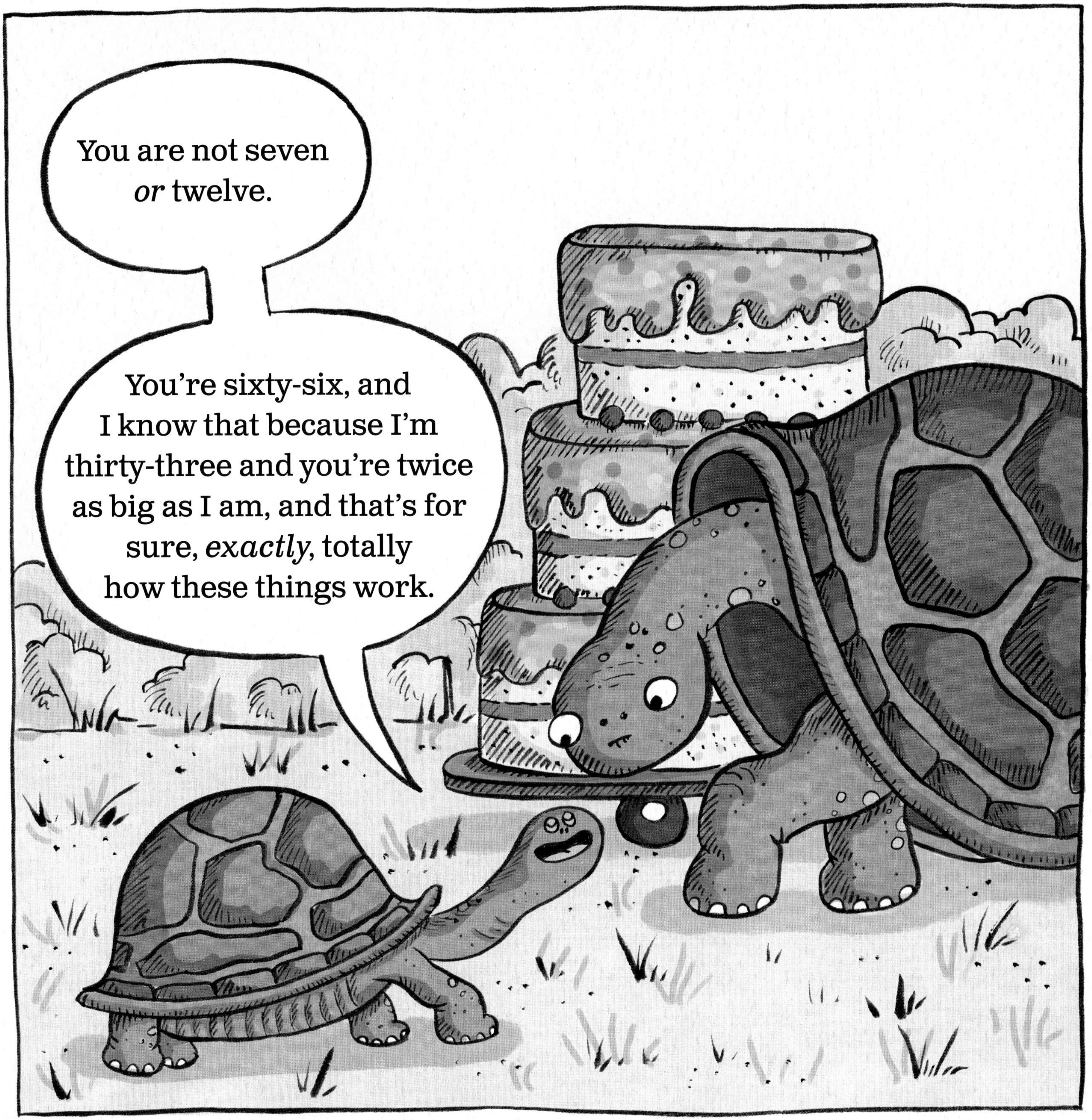
You are not seven *or* twelve.
You're sixty-six, and I know that because I'm thirty-three and you're twice as big as I am, and that's for sure, *exactly*, totally how these things work.

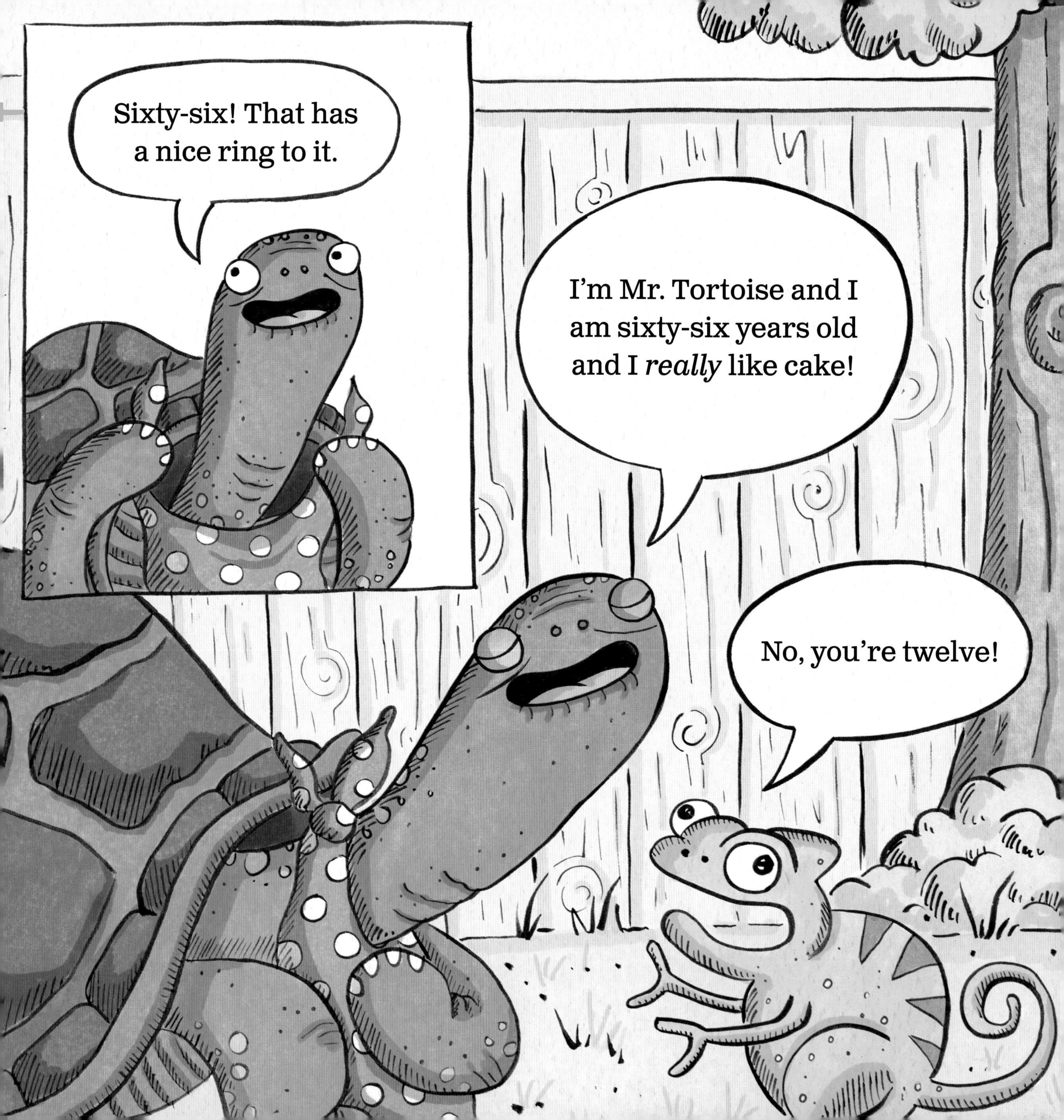
Sixty-six! That has a nice ring to it.
I'm Mr. Tortoise and I am sixty-six years old and I *really* like cake!
No, you're twelve!

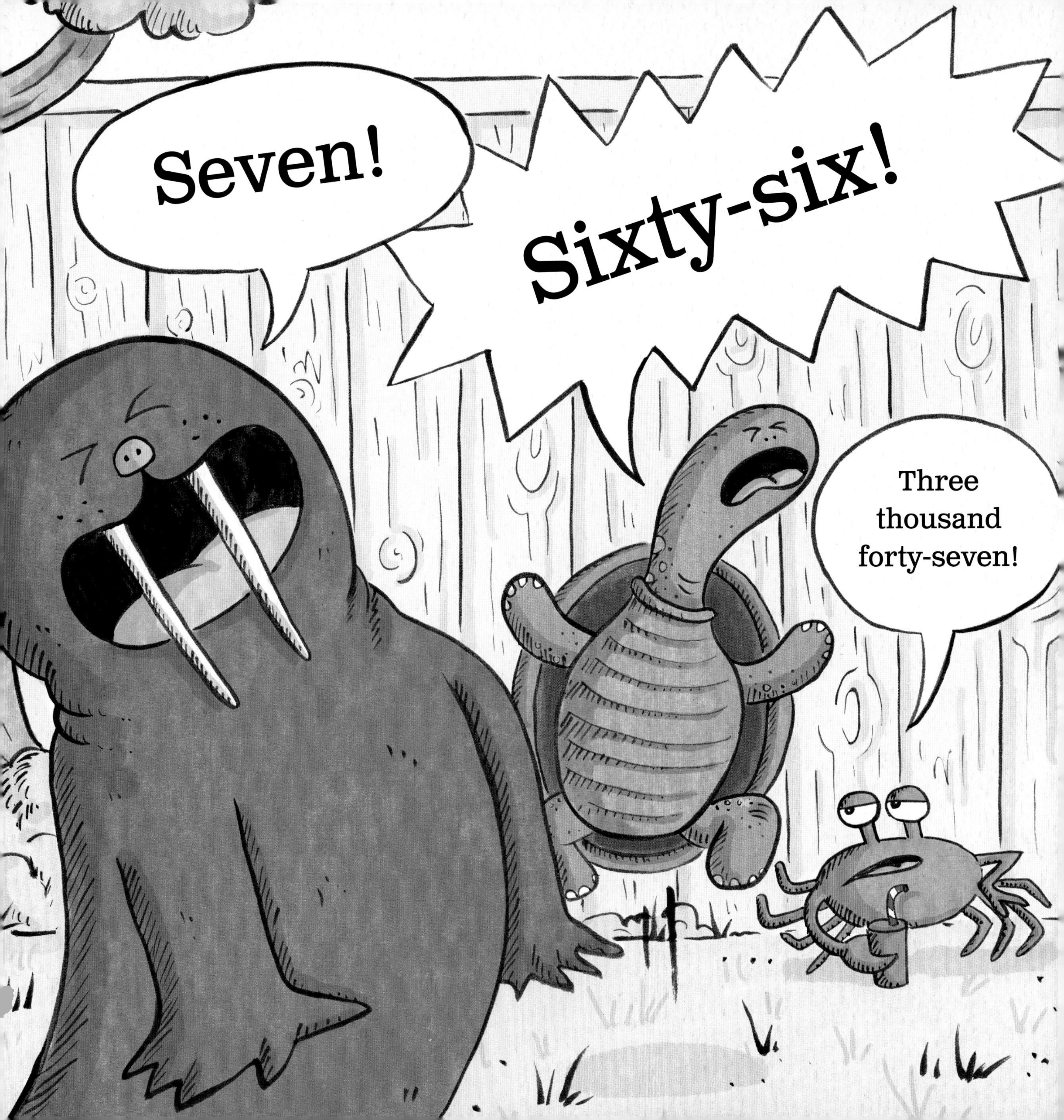
Seven!
Sixty-six!
Three thousand forty-seven!

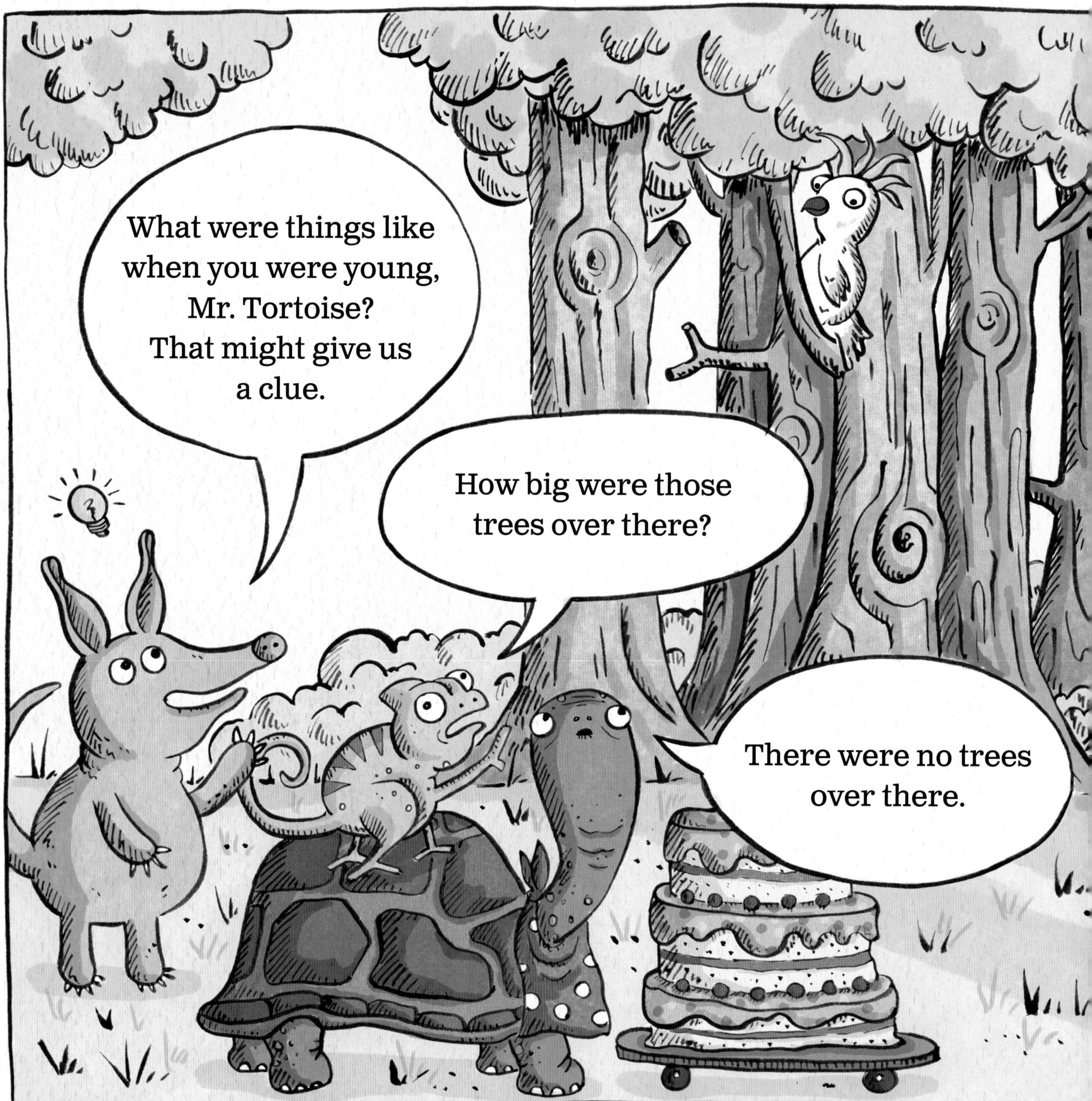
What were things like when you were young, Mr. Tortoise? That might give us a clue.
How big were those trees over there?
There were no trees over there.

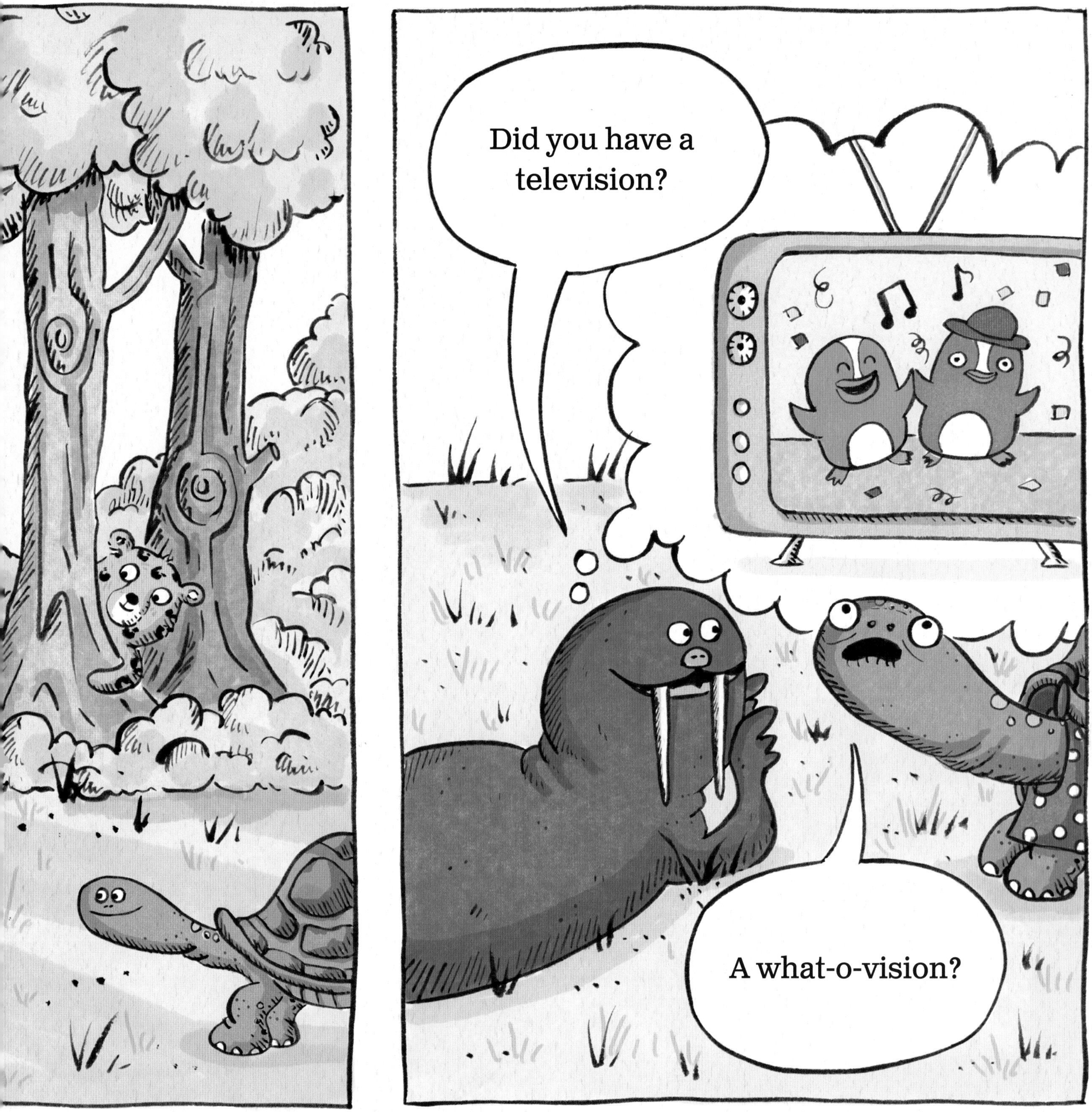
Did you have a television?
A what-o-vision?

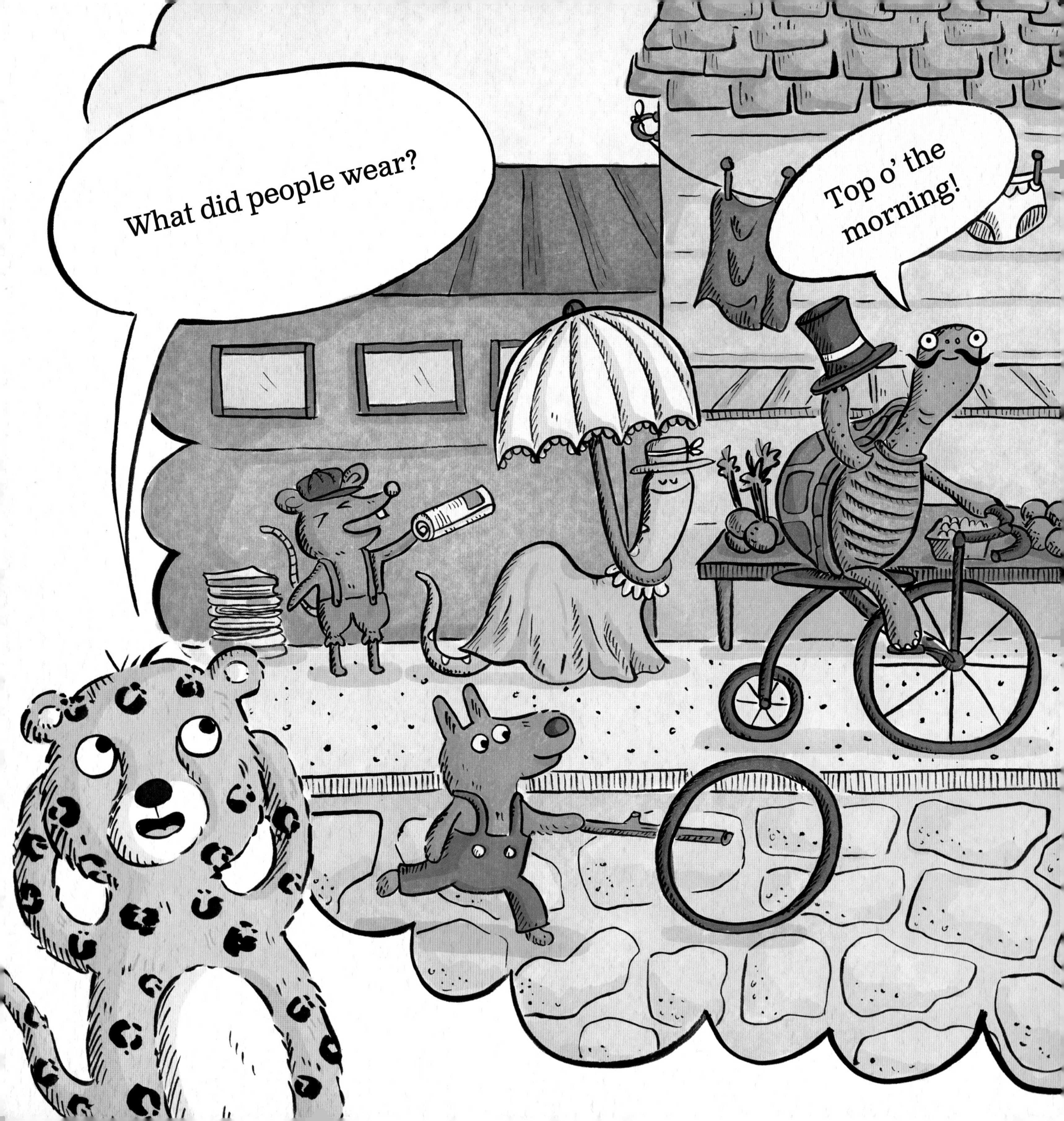
What did people wear?
Top o' the morning!

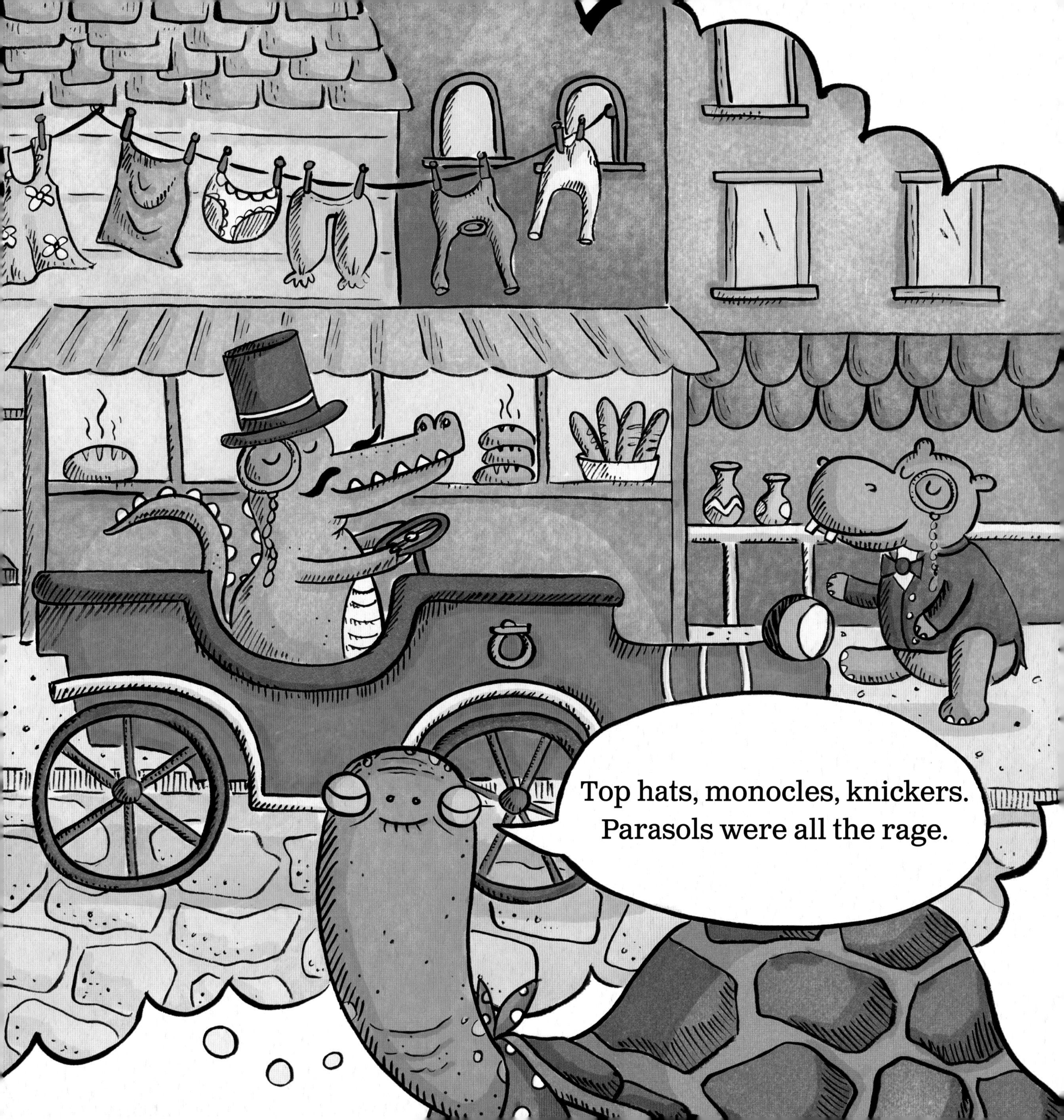
Top hats, monocles, knickers.
Parasols were all the rage.

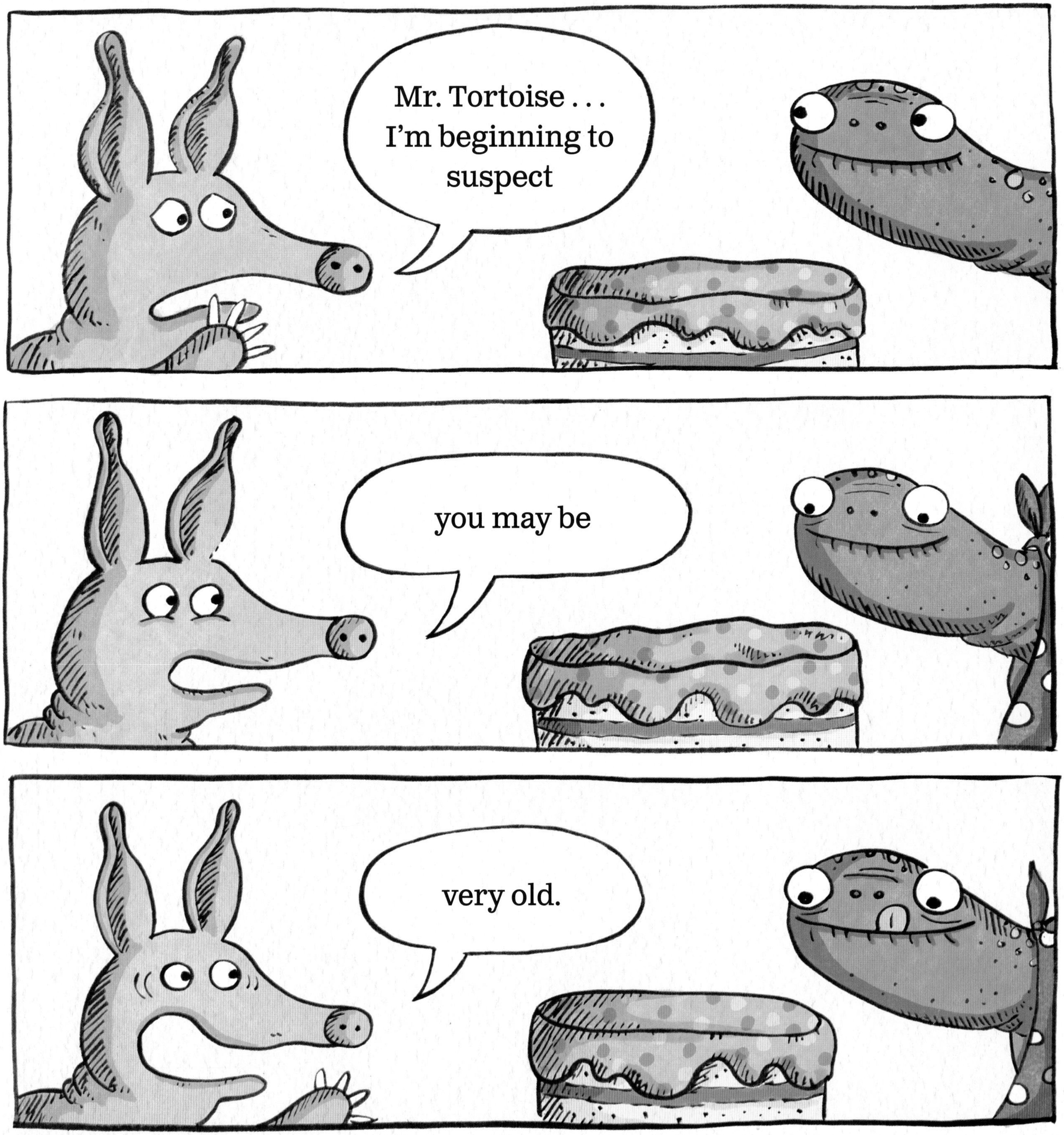
Mr. Tortoise . . . I'm beginning to suspect
you may be
very old.

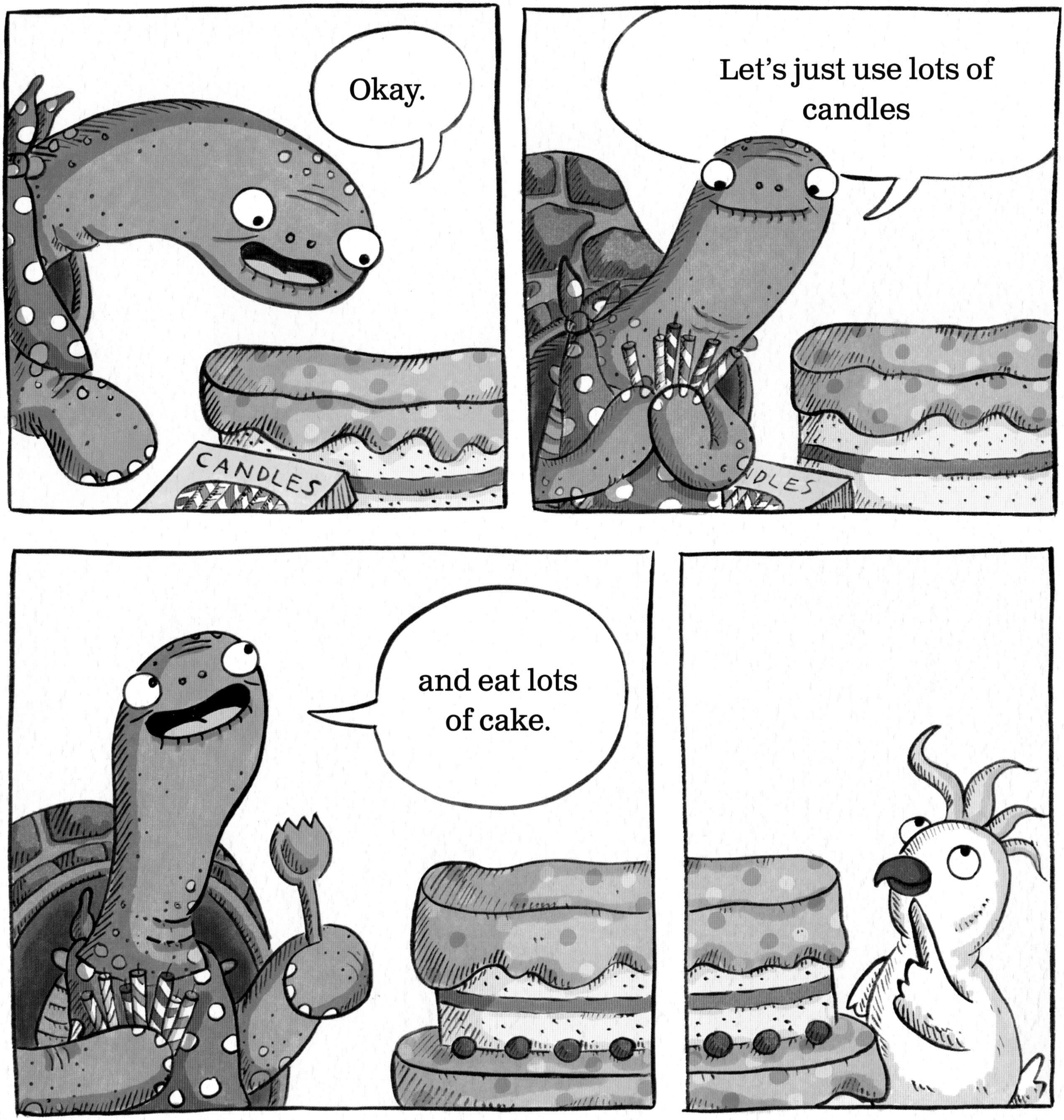
Okay.
CANDLES
Let's just use lots of candles
and eat lots of cake.

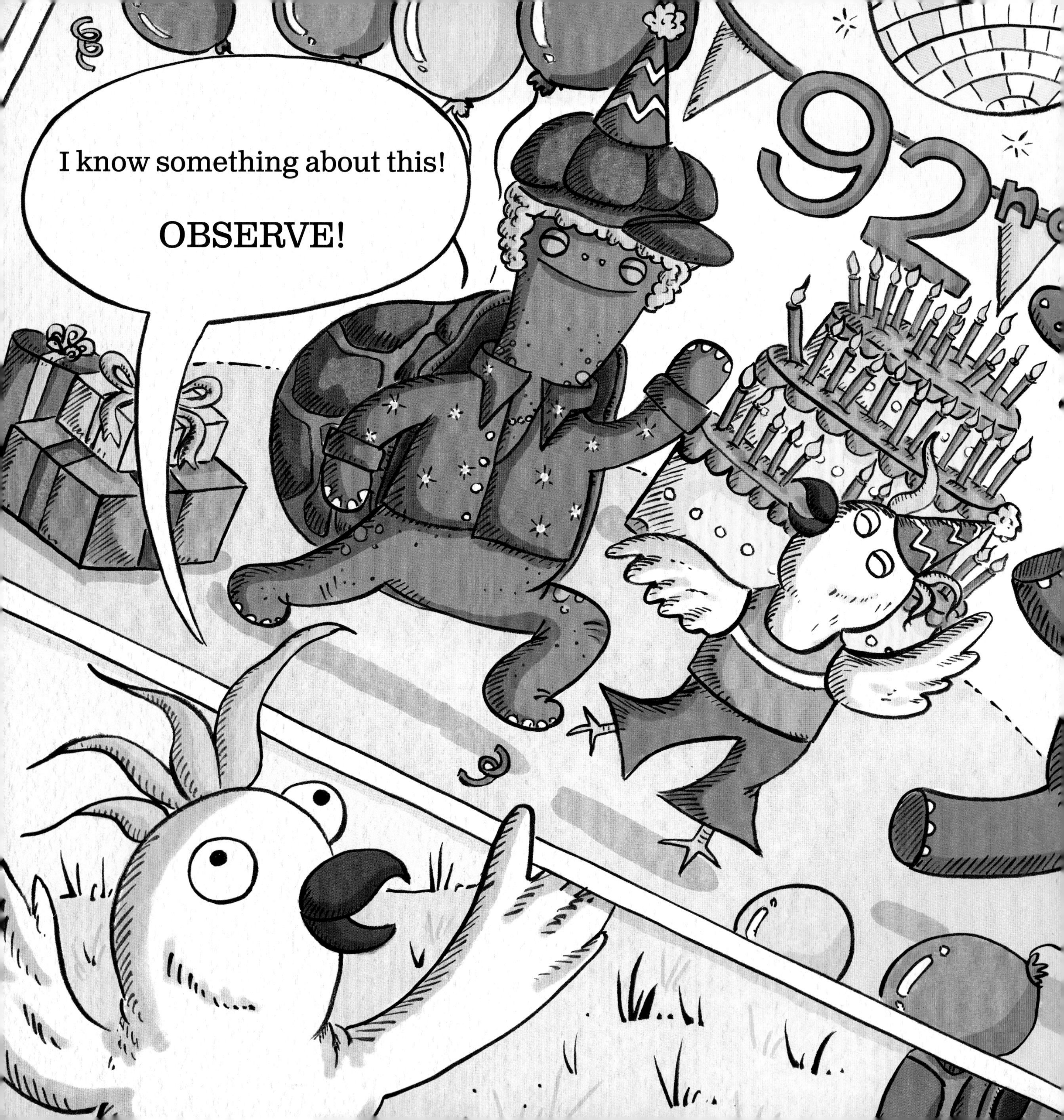
I know something about this!
OBSERVE!
92nd

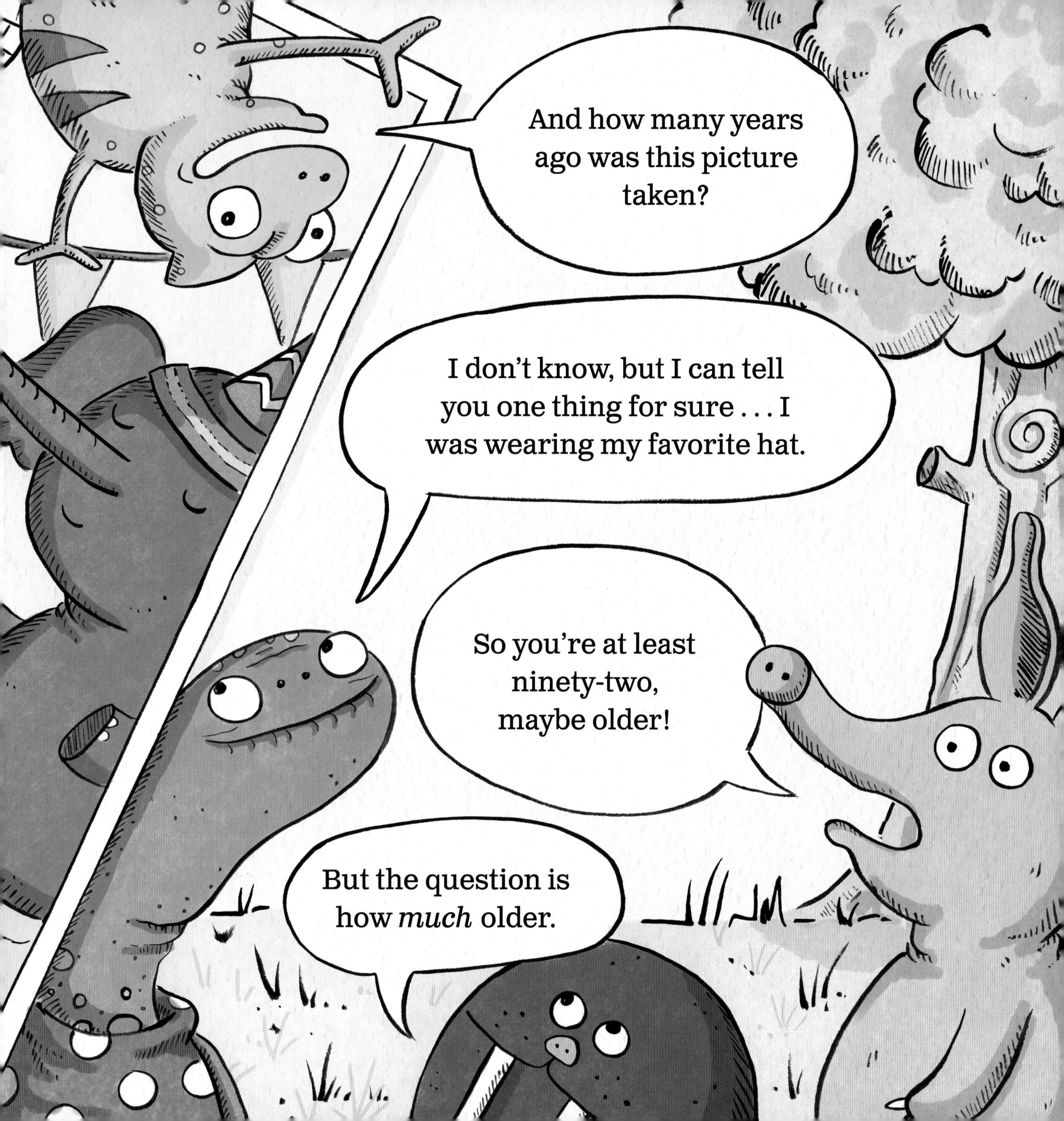
And how many years ago was this picture taken?
I don't know, but I can tell you one thing for sure . . . I was wearing my favorite hat.
So you're at least ninety-two, maybe older!
But the question is how *much* older.

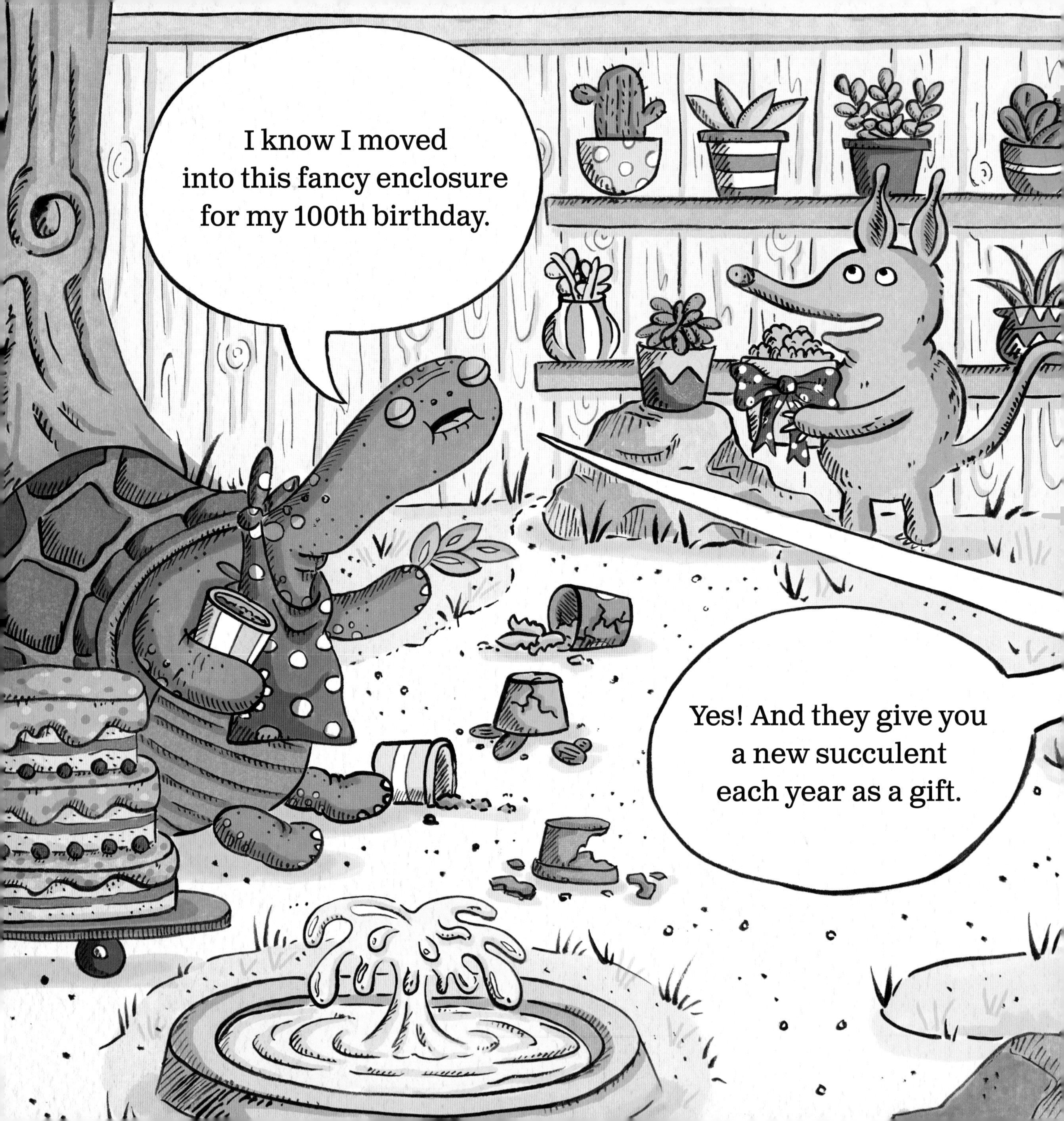
I know I moved into this fancy enclosure for my 100th birthday.
Yes! And they give you a new succulent each year as a gift.

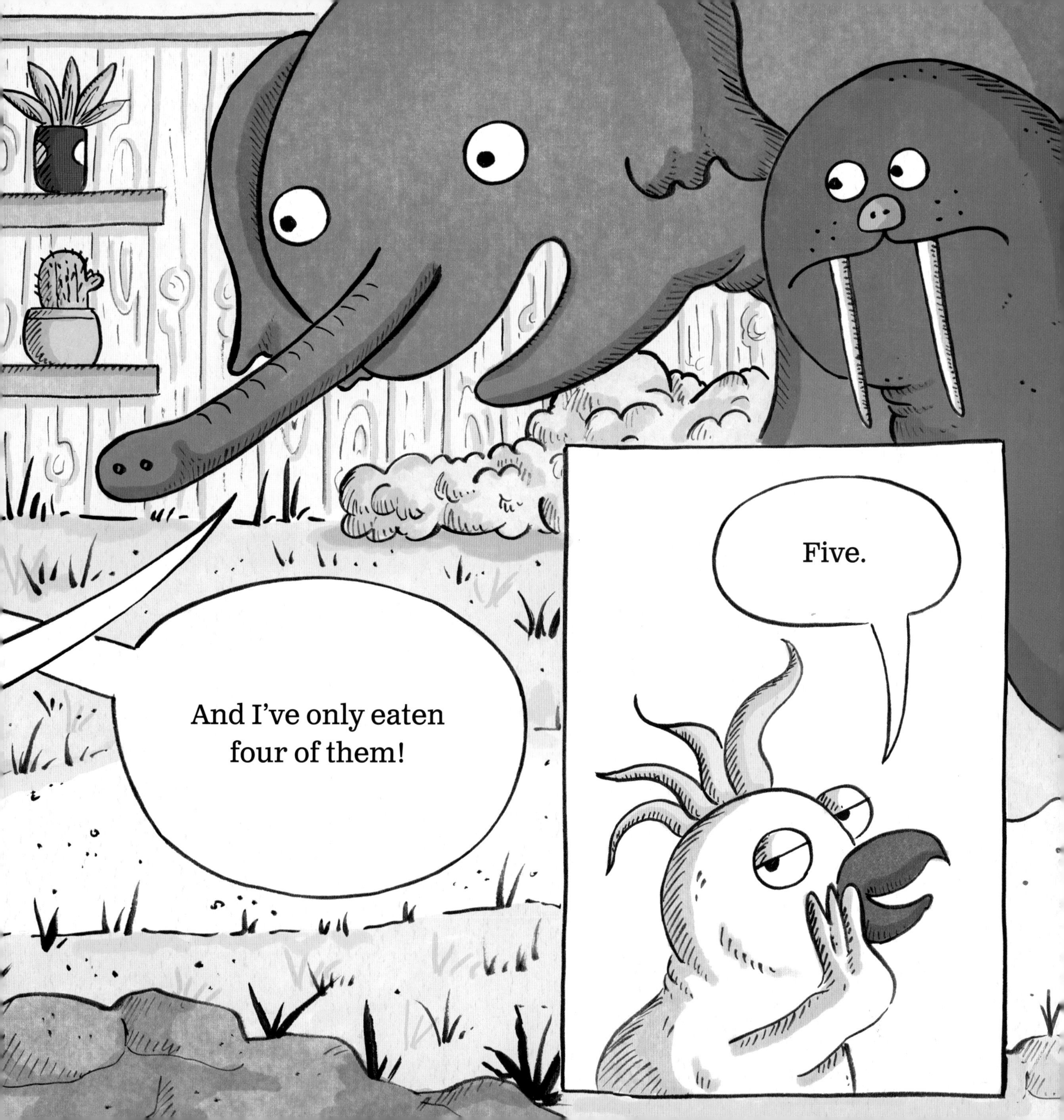
And I've only eaten four of them!
Five.

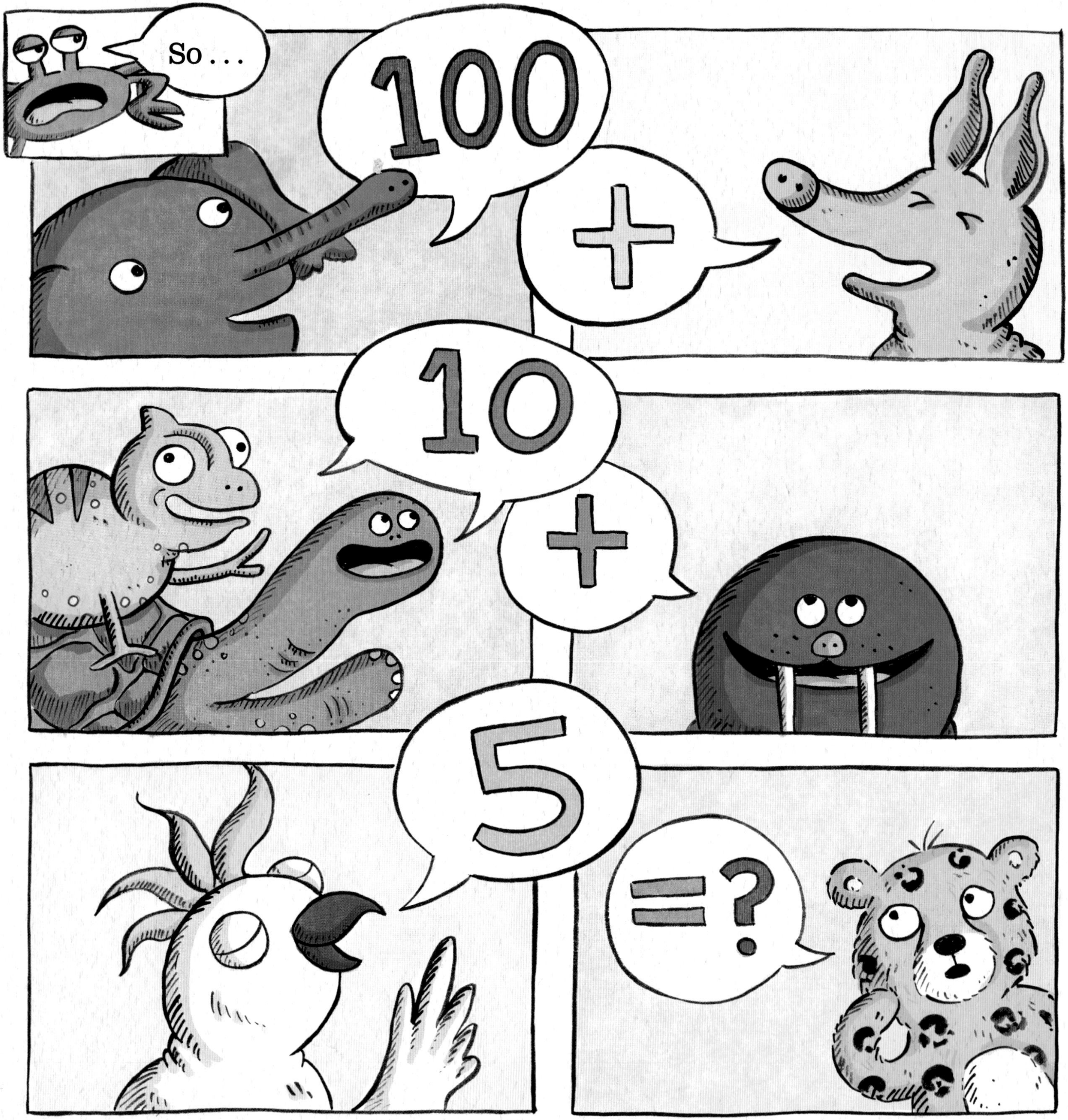
So . . .
100
+
10
+
5
=?

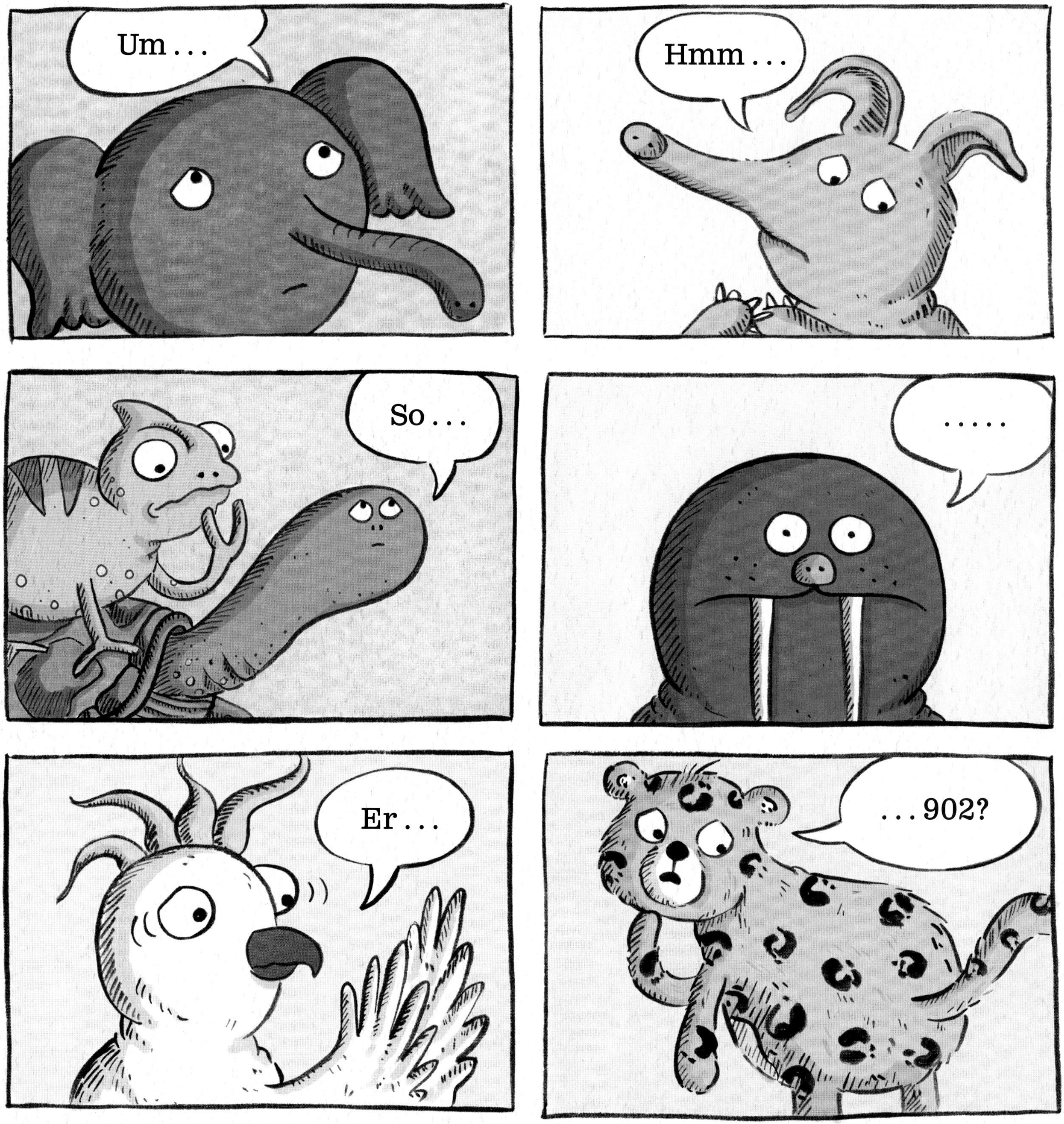
Um . . .
Hmm . . .
So . . .
. . . . .
Er . . .
. . . 902?

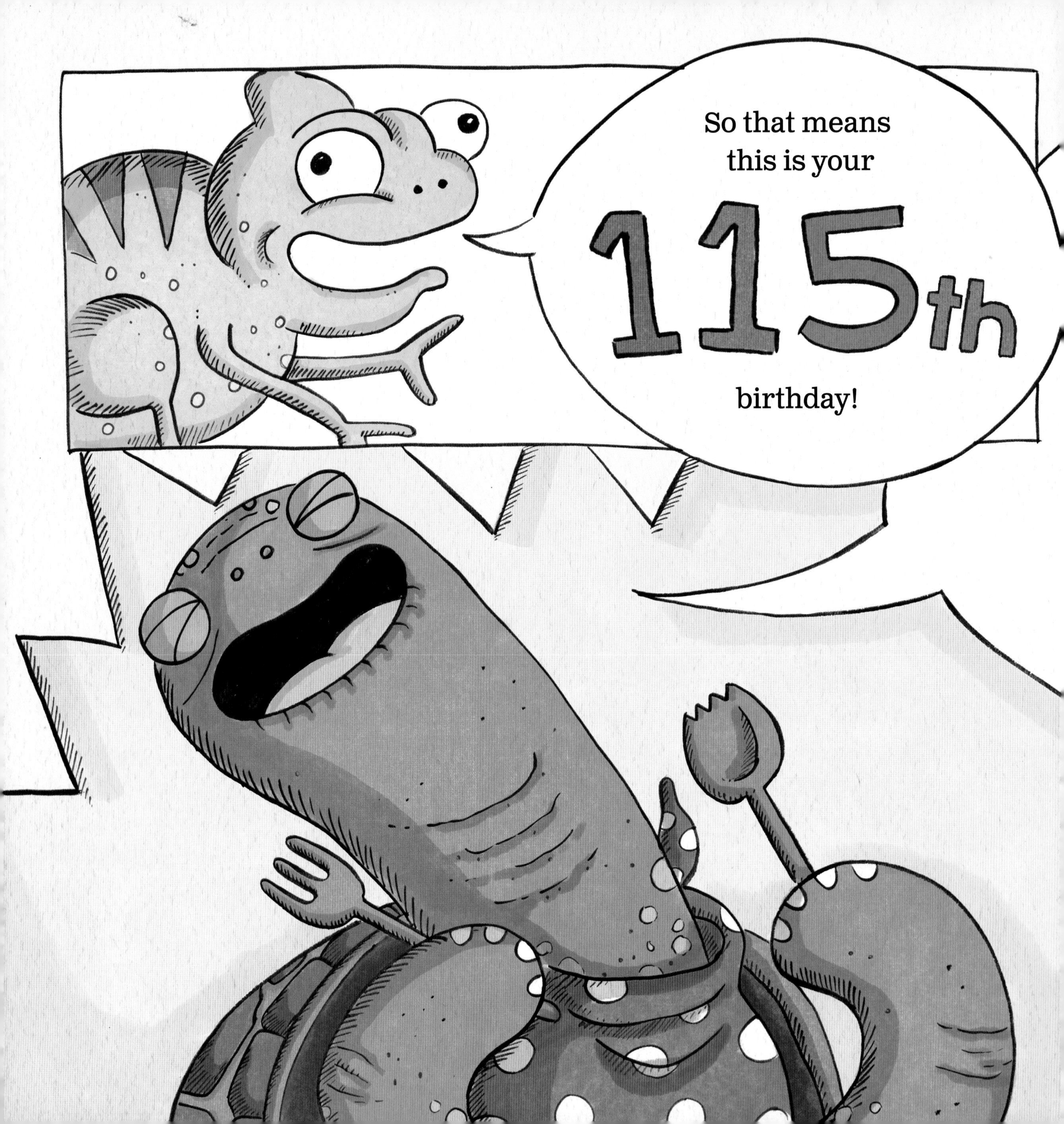
So that means this is your 115th birthday!

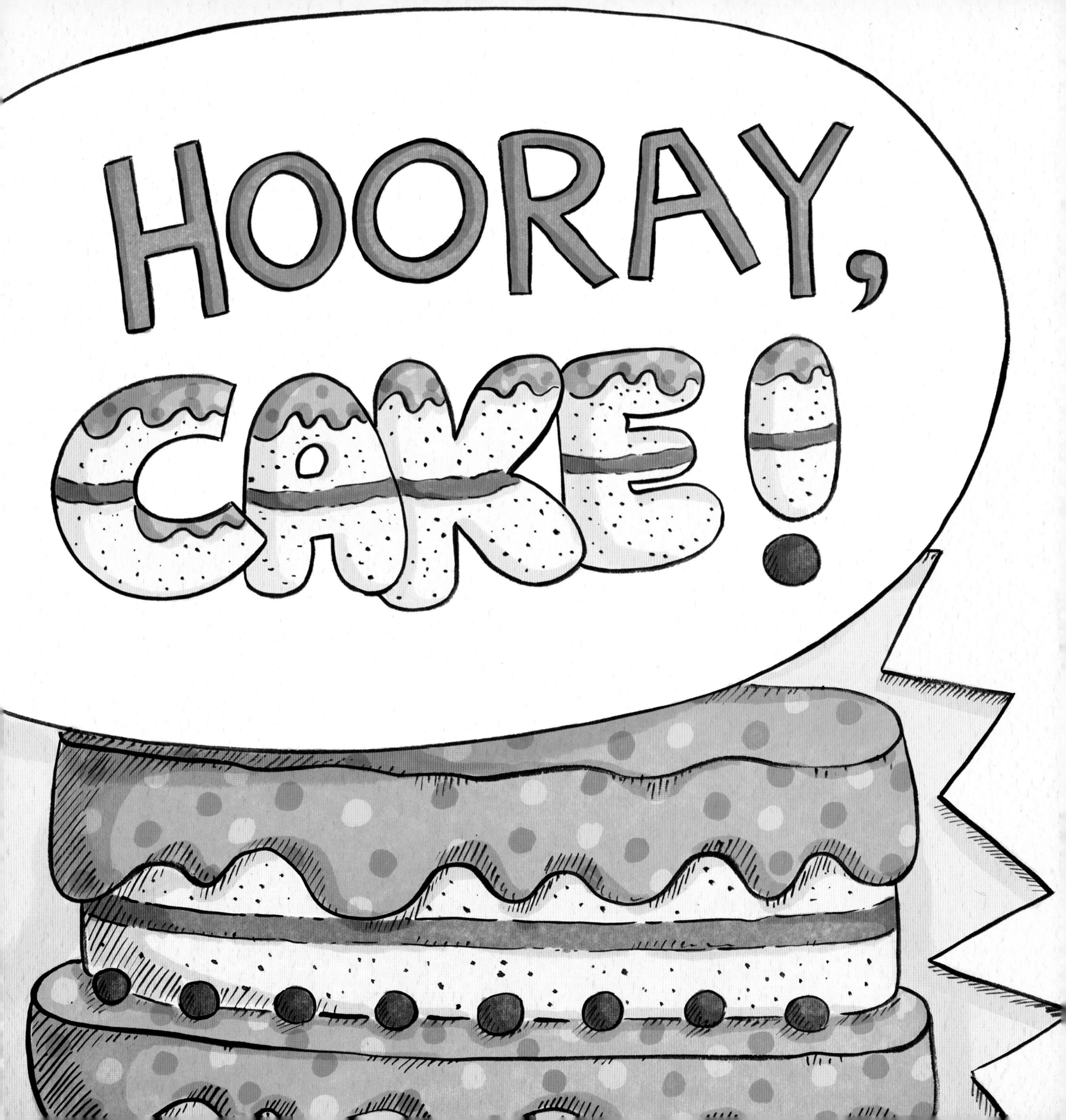
HOORAY, CAKE!

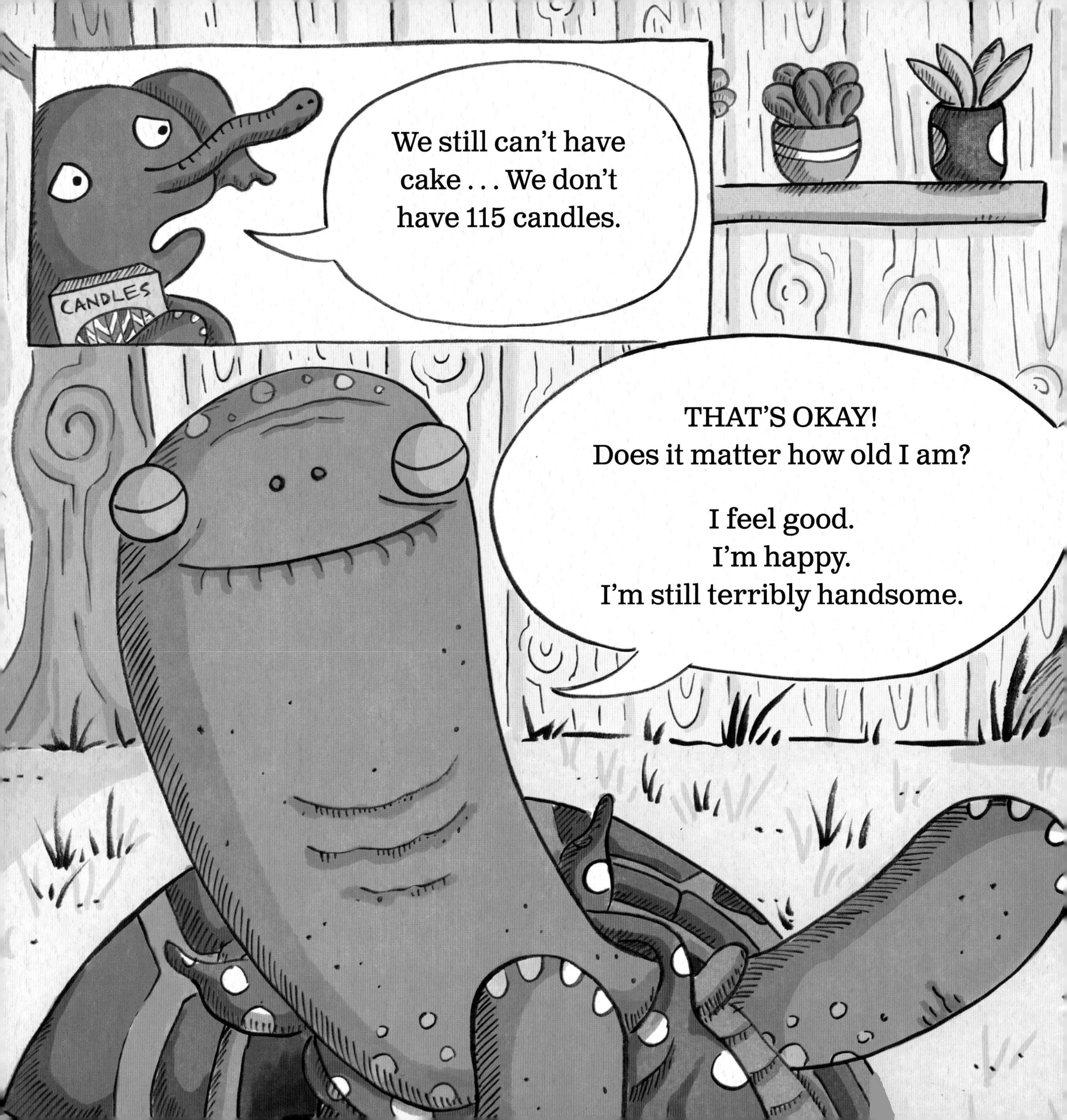

CANDLES
We still can't have cake . . . We don't have 115 candles.
THAT'S OKAY! Does it matter how old I am?
I feel good. I'm happy. I'm still terribly handsome.

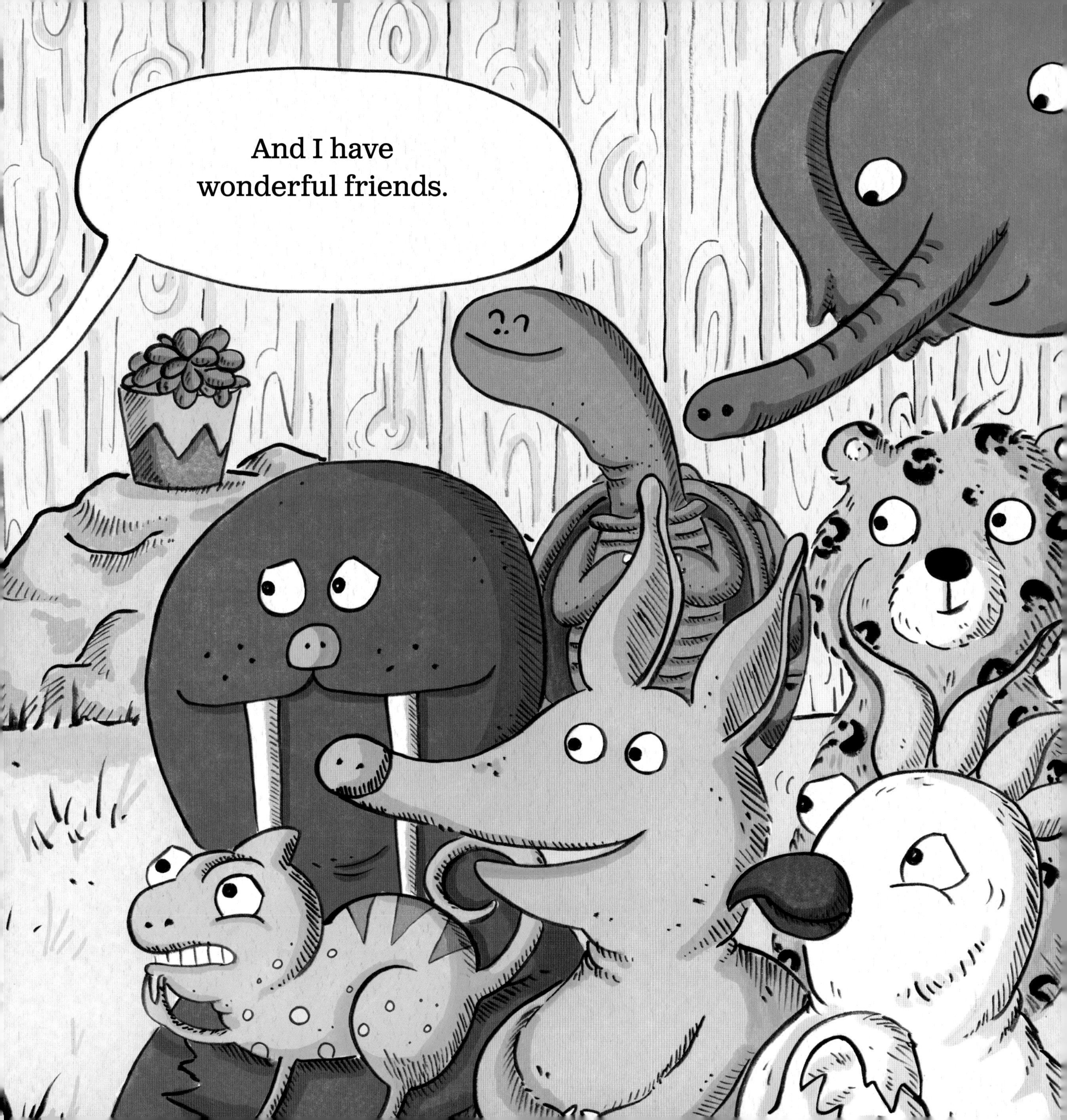
And I have wonderful friends.

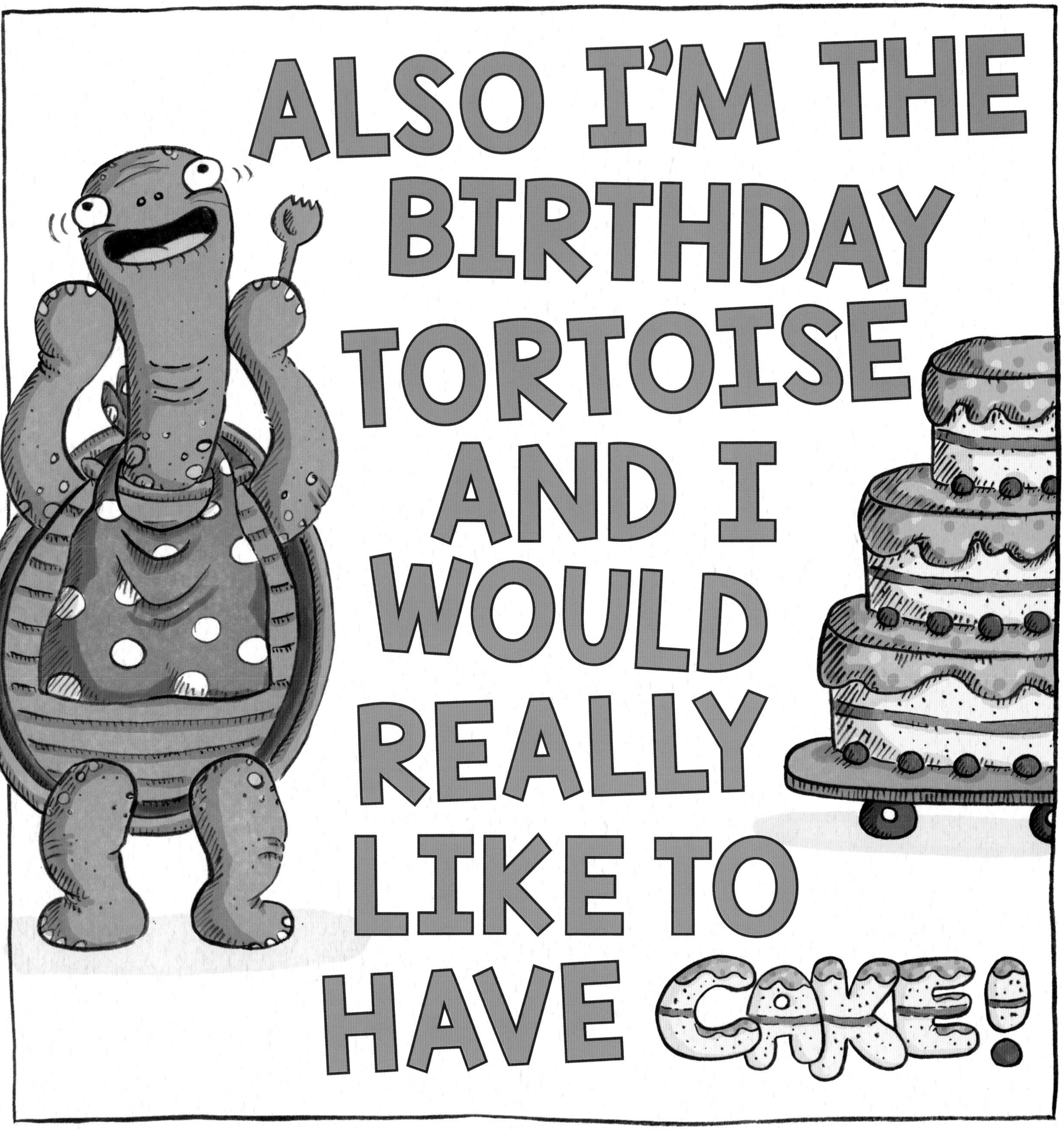
ALSO I'M THE BIRTHDAY TORTOISE AND I WOULD REALLY LIKE TO HAVE CAKE!

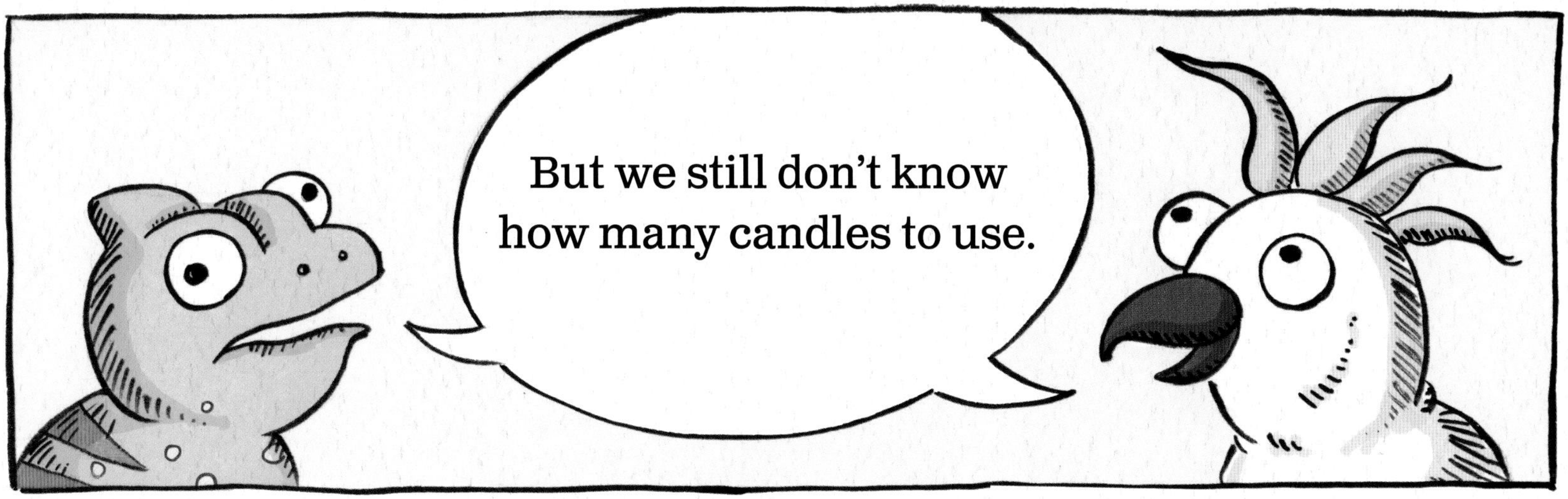
But we still don't know how many candles to use.

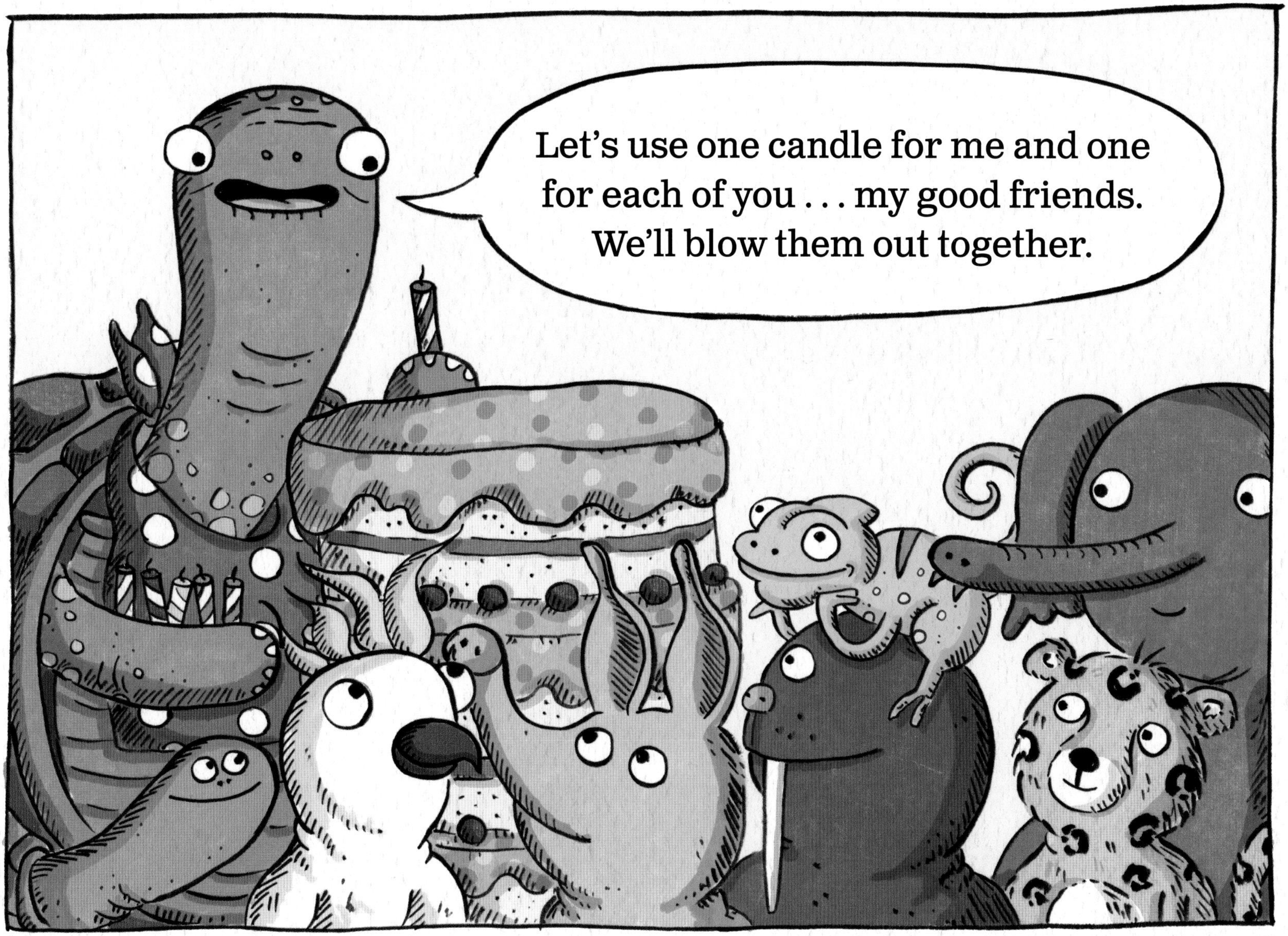
Let's use one candle for me and one for each of you . . . my good friends. We'll blow them out together.

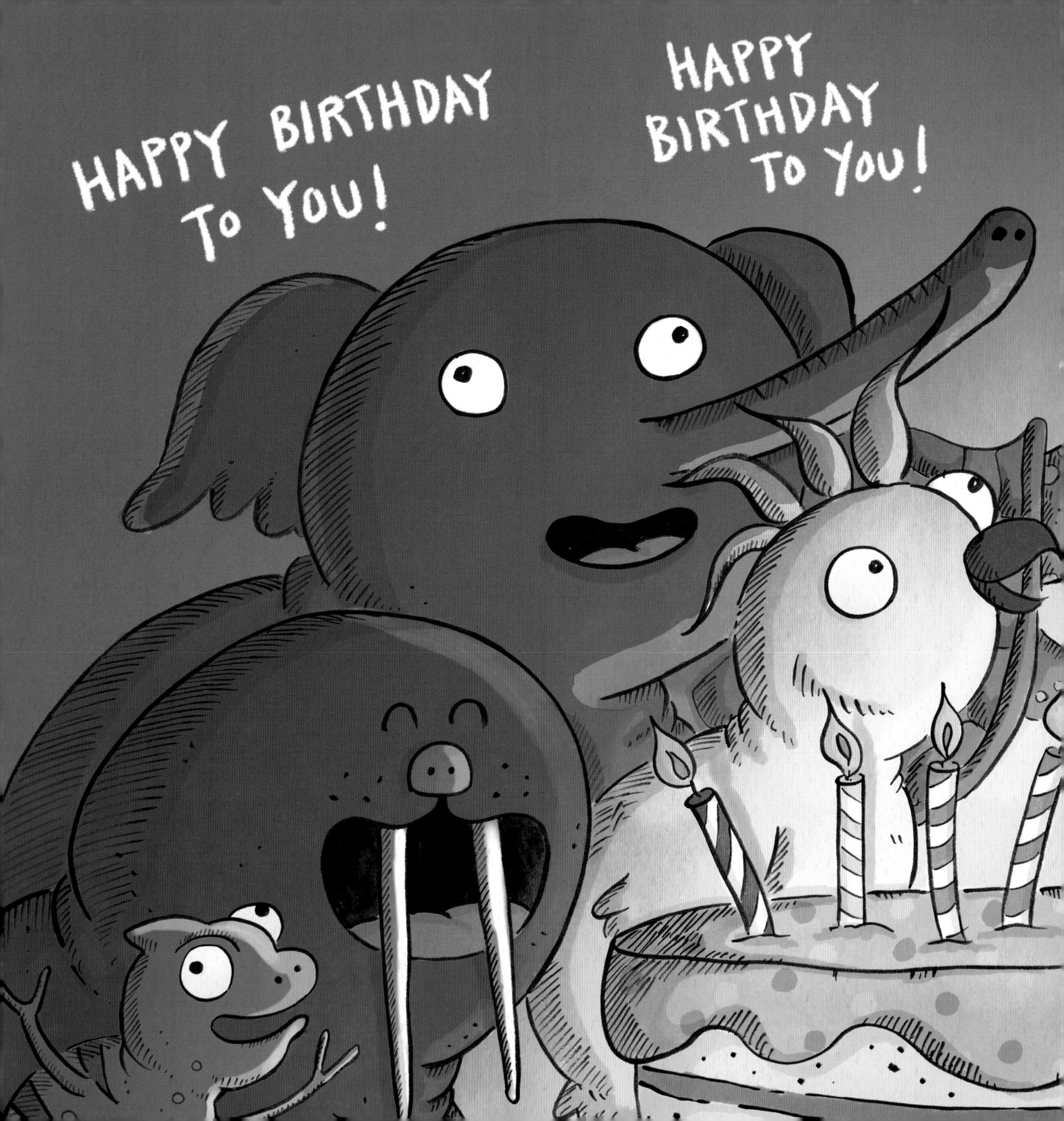
HAPPY BIRTHDAY TO YOU!
HAPPY BIRTHDAY TO YOU!

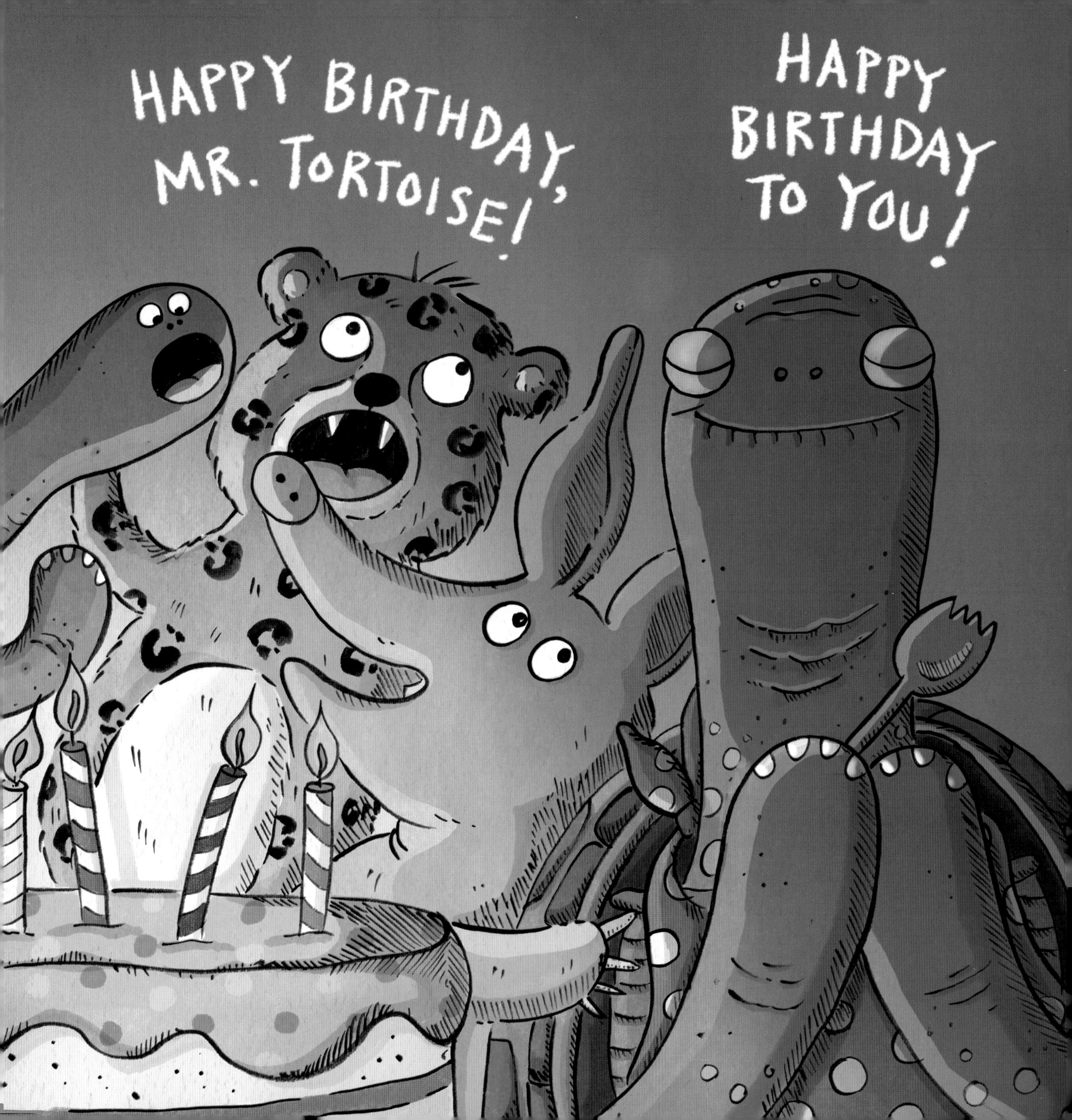
HAPPY BIRTHDAY, MR. TORTOISE!
HAPPY BIRTHDAY TO YOU!

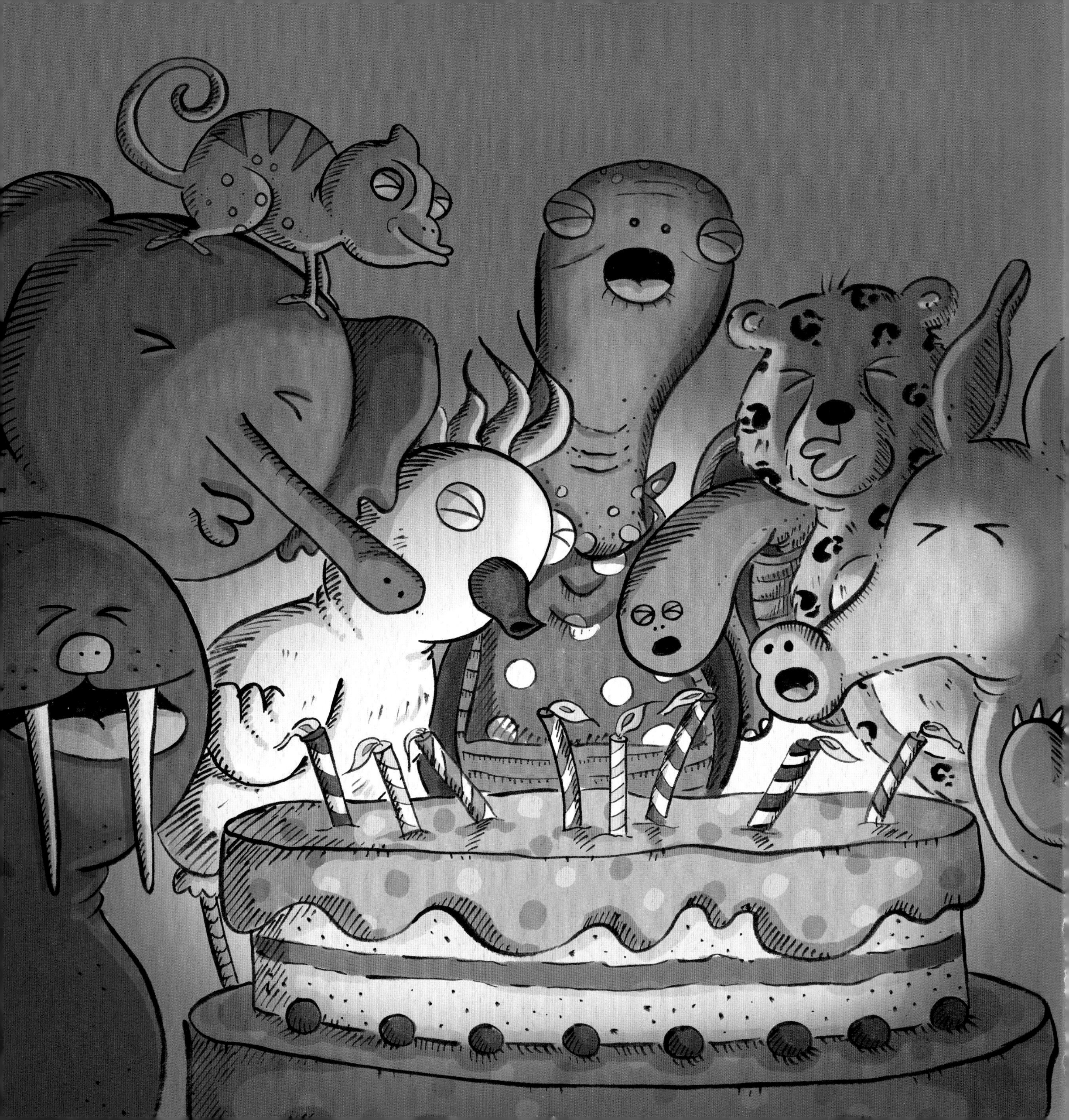

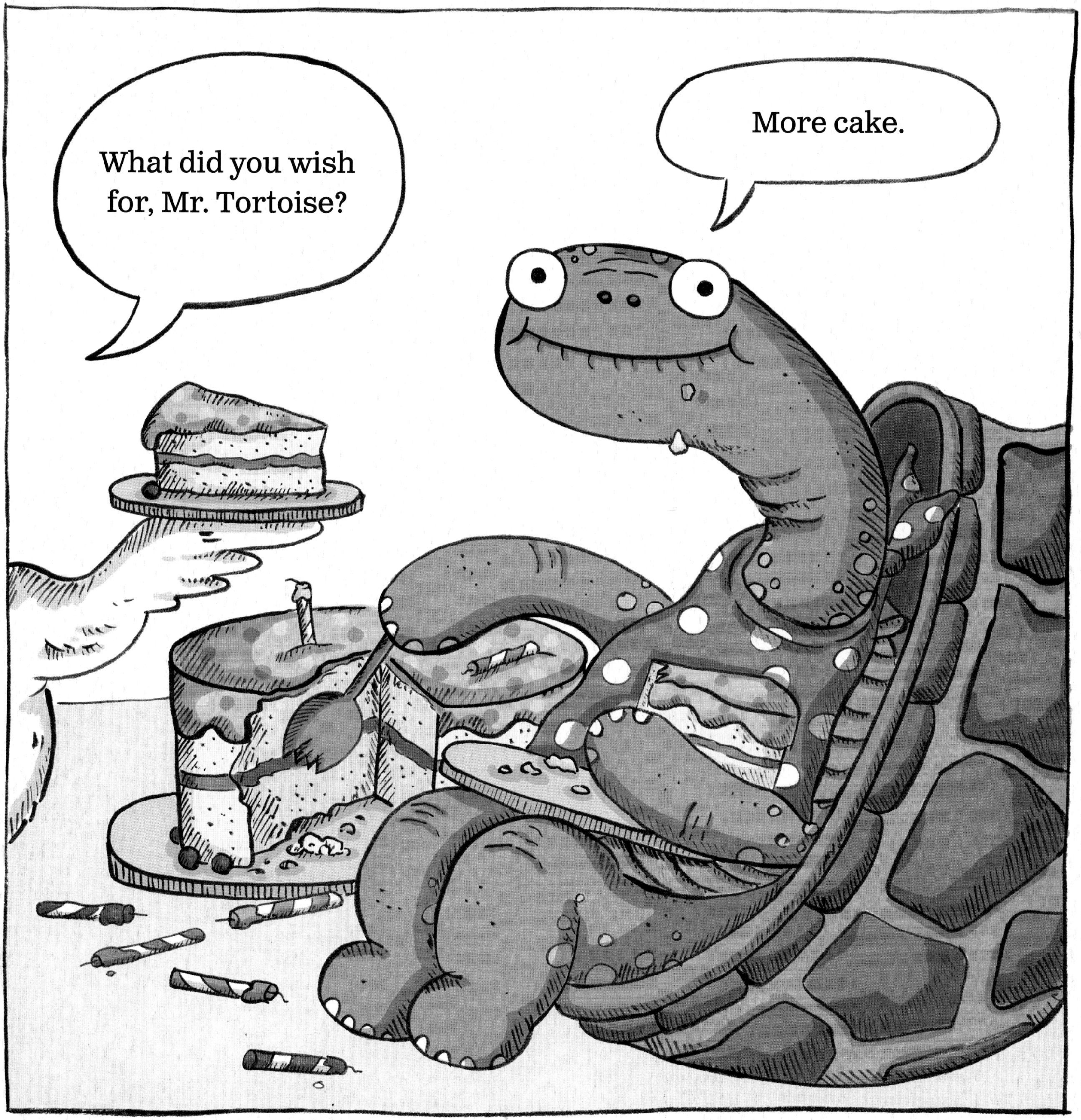
What did you wish for, Mr. Tortoise?
More cake.

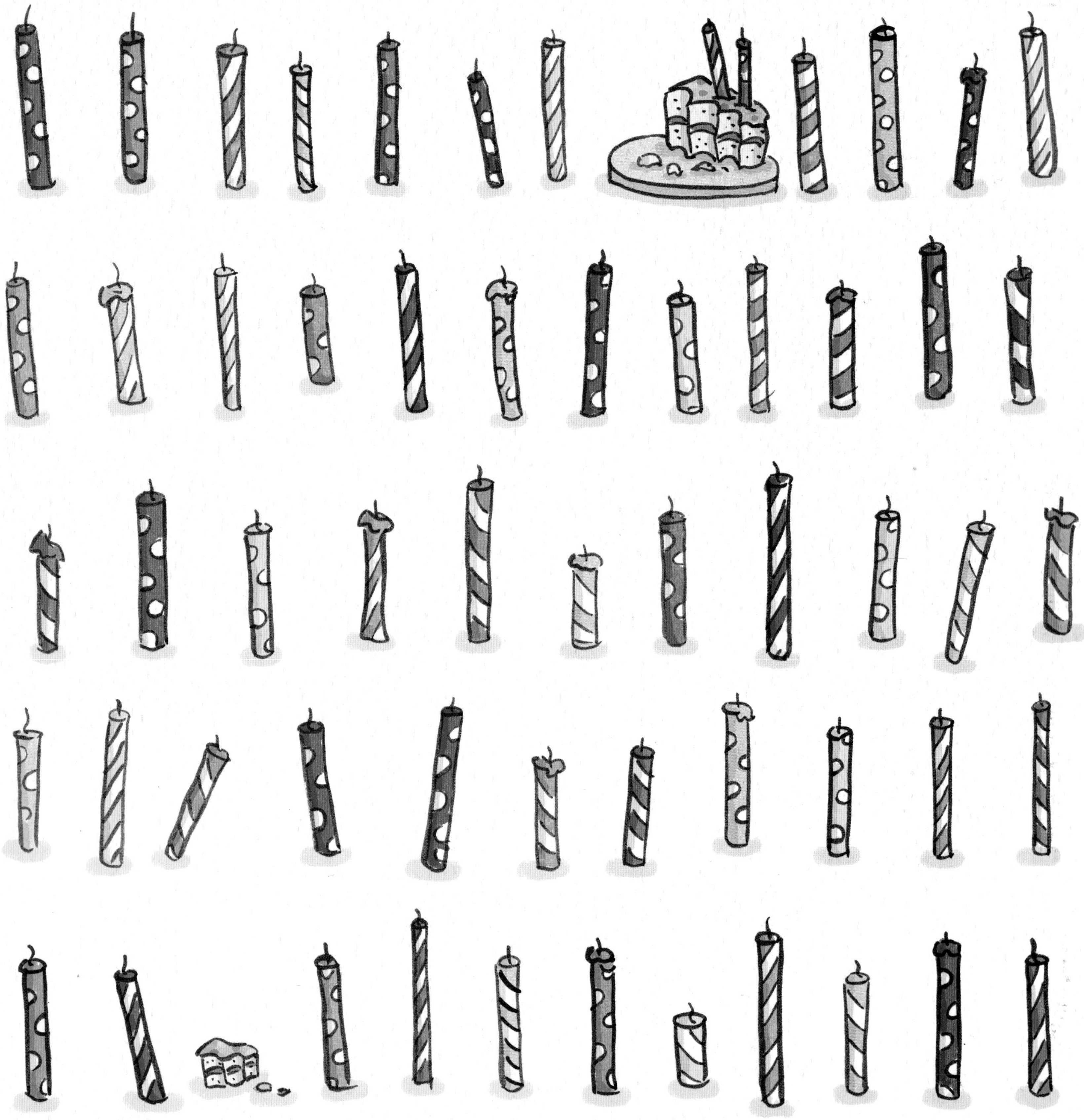